D1794857

ALSO BY AMY L. SAUDER:

*Unfixed*

*I Know You Like a Murder*

# Praise for the Unfixed series:

"Unfixed dug its claws in and isn't letting go anytime soon."

> ~ Emily, book blogger of *Emily S Hurricane*

"This is one with elements you haven't heard but that vibe you crave from the circus. Mysterious, dangerous, and intriguing, this one will captivate you."

> ~ Tabatha, book blogger of *All The Right Reads*

"Virginia Woolf meets Edgar Allan Poe in Amy L. Sauder's stories."

> ~ Kim Kouski, author of *Hidden Secrets* and *The Last Maúl*

"A winding narrative that often hangs somewhere between twisted fairytales like *Pinnochio* and dark whimsy such as Tim Burton."

> ~ Megan Fatheree, author of *Codex*, *The Half-Shape Child*, and the *For Such a Time* series

"This book kept me riveted to the pages and to the twisted fates of each broken, beloved character I met."

> ~ Jennifer Esther Wieland, writer, artist, videographer, and all-around creative

# Picked Up Pieces

## Amy L. Sauder

Book 2 of Unfixed

Cover design by My Lan Khuc Valle (LaolanArt)

Edited by Kate Yelland

Author photograph by Nan Doud (www.nandoud.com)

Fonts: Chunk Five, EB Garamond, Elzevier Caps, Kingthings Widow, Kramer, & Newscast

Copyright © 2025 Amy L. Sauder

All rights reserved

ISBN 978-1-7323530-4-6

Library of Congress Control Number: 2024921241

*For those looking for a resurrection.*

To the readers thinking:
*"Where did we leave the beloved characters again?"*

I'm glad you asked...

Julia is in pieces and with Geppetto's corpse in Dr. Evil's walk-in freezer. The Trenchers and circus crew wait for the strangely-possible miracle of resurrection. Analiese and RaeChaeline—the unlikely murderers who hold that power of resurrection—have inconveniently fled.

The Forgettable is also a corpse, but he doesn't get the cushy freezer resting place. He's still rotting in the circus field just waiting for the wrong person to stumble upon him.

# Prologue

HEN RAECHAELINE HAD DISAPPEARED, the group back at Dr. Evil's wasn't quite clear on what to do. She'd vanished with an odd pronouncement, and they still had two dead bodies to deal with and lives to rebuild. Two stories intersecting without competing is a feat, so how could all these intertwining stories head the same direction?

"You'd do best to rally the troops to find her," Dr. Evil said to no one in particular. "Everything is hanging on it."

"She's the most impossible to find," Nick said. "You know that."

The man known as Dr. Evil didn't stick around to hear, though. He had his own solution in the back.

Viel opened the freezer and approached the corpse. Felt his pulse, again, habit more than hope. He touched the eyelids tentatively and spread them open. Gep's blank lifeless gaze stared back. Of course.

Not particularly one to wait for a miracle, Viel pushed Gep up with strength you wouldn't suspect. He gripped under his arms and pulled, and Gep crashed to the floor. That would hurt if Gep ever lived again to feel it.

Viel lugged the body down the hall and nudged the flimsy door open. He propped Gep up against himself as best he could, though with Gep's body being his own weight plus half, Viel was about to collapse. He was determined, though. If Gep wouldn't walk out of this building alive, then Viel would take matters into his own hands and get Gep to walk out of this building dead. RaeChaeline hadn't thought to specify. Who would?

So he scooted along with Gep in front and hoped it counted as walking. He kicked Gep's left and then right foot up for good measure.

It only took a few inches distance; at least, he suspected. Finally, outside the building, Viel pushed Gep off of him and into the bushes.

That'll do.

Sometimes you gotta give prophecy a helping hand.

# -10

AECHAELINE ISN'T ONE TO LEAVE a mess behind. She'd handled—hopefully—Julia and Gep's resurrection earlier. But there was still one other body needing her words.

It would be more tricky, only knowing his false name and his connection to Max, nothing else. As she drove, she rehearsed carefully in her mind what words might help—Max's roommate...? No. The man known as Ferguson...? No. No idea if people knew him as that. The man whose ID said Ferguson E. Tibble. That. Super specific.

Then, she opened her mouth, forming the words with her tongue silently to practice. She only needed to tie the sentence to herself in some way now. She whispered in hope, "As I approach his body, the man whose ID said Ferguson E. Tibble will rise..." As she turned onto the road past the barley field, though, her words twisted, as they're wont to do.

Ferguson's body did rise, but not on its own. Police lights flashed and crime scene tape fluttered in the breeze. A stretcher was raised, with his still very much dead body on it, and placed in a van. Her stomach clenched, and she gritted her teeth. She drove past without slowing.

RaeCh didn't know where she was going, or what it would help. Once again, the gift Gep had bestowed on her was too much to bear, too much to grapple with. It was enough to resurrect him—hopefully—to give them a second chance, but it also doubled the chances of their destruction. So she ran, much like Analiese, knowing it prevented nothing, knowing she was simultaneously helpless and powerful beyond imagination.

Meanwhile, Analiese returned, helpless and powerful beyond imagination. Though it took a moment for others to notice…

## -9

E STAY RIGHT HERE with Julia," Mrs. Trencher insisted. Max interjected. "I'm going to find Fancy. You all do what you want."

"Don't rush off too quickly," Analiese said from the doorway.

The room quieted as eyes turned to see her.

"Quite a mess you've created," Mrs. Trencher muttered as she backed to the far side of the room. "Can't live with the consequences, so you run. How predictable."

Analiese refused to dignify that with a response. "Nick. You're free now. Let's get out of here."

"Oh, you're here for Nick," Max said. "I see how it is. Always about Nick."

"We have a deal," Analiese said.

"We have Julia," Nick implored. "Help her?"

Analiese smoothed her shirt as if it was wrinkled and sniffed. "Is she..." She paused. "Is she salvageable? Can she recover?"

"That's what we're all wondering," Nick said. "I mean, it could be 'the end', right?"

"Don't say it," Analiese warned.

Mr. Trencher jolted out of his seat. "We need Sylas! He would know."

For once, Mrs. Trencher and Nick agreed with each other, and frowned.

"Sylas?" Analiese said.

"He sees how things work." Mr. Trencher bobbed his head. "Truly fascinating!"

"It's only circus tricks," Mrs. Trencher brushed aside.

Analiese pursed her lips. "Only circus tricks." She walked around the desk, touching the papers that were scattered across it. "Quite a surprise to see you all sitting so comfortably in Dr. Evil's lair. I think I'd call it more careless than brave."

"Dr..." Mr. Trencher coughed. "Dr. *Evil* you say?"

"It's a pet name," she brushed him off. "More appropriate term than that 'Dr. Wise' that locked Nick up."

"Wise is his real name," Mr. Trencher corrected. "Not a pet name."

"Uh huh."

Analiese tapped her hands on the desk, then smoothed its top and walked to the back to find Julia. "I don't need another circus trick," she called back and waved her hand. "I have my own."

She peeked in the first door (bathroom), then the second (closet)...you get the idea. Finally she came to the fourth door—the freezer. She hadn't yet seen Gep's dead body, and wasn't sure she was ready. Any dead body was difficult, especially Julia's, but she wasn't ready to see Gep's. And yet...

She opened the door, braced herself for the chill of the freezer and the chill of what she'd see. Two tables stood parallel, and she approached the first, refusing to look to the second. Each piece of

Julia's body was laid out in order on a table, just waiting for the right skills to put her together.

But the words she hadn't cared about came back to her. Gep had said "that's the end," and now she hoped it wasn't. She shuddered and grasped a finger. "You won't ever hear me say this," she whispered, "but I'm sorry."

Analiese instinctively looked at the second table, as if Gep could hear.

She froze. Not because of the chill in the room. Because the second table was empty.

Her eyes widened, and she glanced around the room. She was alone with Julia. Her heart picked up its pace, and her face grew warm. Suddenly a freezer wasn't cold enough.

"She didn't do it," she said out loud, hoping hearing the words would bring the reassurance her thoughts couldn't. "It's preposterous. Impossible. He's just been moved...somewhere..."

# -8

AX WOULD WANT TO KNOW, RaeChaeline thought. And now, what with Ferguson still dead and off to the morgue, she couldn't just whisk him off to tell Max everything's dandy.

She should just leave Max hanging, really, and yet she didn't want to be that type of person. She *hoped* she wasn't that type of person.

So to will that into being, she had to get a message to Max. But how?

She had already decided people were less likely to talk about her if she wasn't around. And people were less likely to talk about her if she wasn't a messenger.

No, she couldn't see Max. He wasn't clever enough to bear the weight of her present circumstances. She couldn't trust his words.

This wasn't her problem. It really wasn't. She was supposed to be focused on Gep.

And yet...she couldn't shake that if she had the power to do something here, she probably should. A mishap is just an opportunity, something you can always come back from.

Grappling with two competing curses (or gifts, depending on the day and moment), she needed to become someone else, just for a little while. Hopefully.

She couldn't go back to the crime scene—the car was a dead giveaway. The cops would be swarming, itching for anything to peg as evidence…

RaeChaeline smiled. There's an idea. If she could catch a break at the police station, there was a chance. A small one, but it was something.

RaeChaeline did catch a break at the police station. She waltzed in like she owned the place and left with her very own souvenir. Given time, anything can happen when ya set your mind to it.

It didn't take long to drive from the police station to the coroner's office. She entered wearing the police jacket she'd managed to snag—using her old gift from Gep instead of the new one—and she quickly said "hello" to catch attention. She'd learned early that her voice could change perceptions, and she didn't need it to blow her cover after one had already been set.

"Oh, hi! What ya here for this time?" the receptionist said.

RaeChaeline slipped into character easily after years of practice, though there was a persistent knot in her stomach insisting *this time* would be the time she's found out. "I'm here for the John Doe."

"Ahh, he's just arrived." And without further question, the receptionist led her past the foyer. RaeChaeline made a mental note to keep the jacket handy. Never know when ya need this costume.

The receptionist opened the door of a closed-off room and gestured toward the body.

RaeChaeline cleared her throat. "You didn't...do anything to it yet. Did you?"

The receptionist smiled, a mix of amusement and understanding. "No, just as it was discovered for now."

"Good. I'm uhmm, gonna need a moment alone. Make sure we cross all our T's, ya know."

The receptionist gestured at a box on a shelf. "Use gloves if you touch anything. You know the drill."

RaeChaeline nodded. Assuredness had to be part of the act and she'd already seen that slip with the previous question.

The receptionist returned to her perch, and RaeChaeline had the run of the place. At least, for a moment. She paced and thought. She couldn't have her words twist again. She tentatively approached the body. She didn't *like* appearing so comfortable with dead bodies, but that was the cost of murder she supposed.

She studied this man, who would in some way take her memories when—if—he awoke. Who would probably have trouble walking out of this building without causing a scandal—at least, for as long as they would have memory of him. Even if it was possible, there was no convenient way to bring him to life. Life was never convenient. This ability she had was never convenient.

The best option would be to tie his life to the absence of others. And so, she tried these words on for size. Hoping. "When I and all other...living humans...are gone from this property, the man who..." she couldn't say the man who has the ID. That's probably currently Max. How did she say it before? "...the man whose ID says Ferguson E. Tibble will come back to life." She only hoped no one else had stolen his identity recently.

She nodded satisfactorily, her work here done. At least, she would hope. At any rate, she'd done a nice thing for Max. She could move on to her own problems, or Gep's in this case.

As she was leaving, a curious man was at reception. He was tapping his fingers on the desk, and the receptionist was smiling, apologizing, looking around the room. When her eyes caught RaeChaeline's, she lit up. "Oh hey," she said to the man. "Wait here a moment. Let me check again."

She briskly approached RaeChaeline. "This man," she gestured her head his direction, "has been visiting daily asking if we found a Jane Doe in the circus lot. And obviously, this isn't a Jane Doe. But it is curious."

"Huh. It *is* curious." RaeChaeline looked him over. She didn't recognize him. What was he after? Julia would be the only dead lady, unless he's looking for a live one—Phoebe, Analiese, or just some woman who attended the circus that night, then ran off to a better life without him, perhaps. She didn't have time for this, but she also couldn't have this guy getting in her way. So... "I'll take him in, ask some questions, make sure everything's on the up and up. Who knows, maybe it's all innocent and I can help him find whoever he's looking for."

The receptionist nodded and smiled. "Perfect." She walked back to the man. "Sylas. I think I have someone here who can help."

Sylas looked over and sized her up. "You work all right, I suppose."

RaeChaeline's brows furrowed. "I'm not going to thank you for that vote of confidence. Let's go."

Then, as they turned to leave, RaeChaeline remembered. "Oh, the body! John Doe. Don't touch him today at least. Maybe tomorrow. Wait 'til I get in touch."

The receptionist nodded. RaeChaeline and Sylas both had hoped to leave with a different person, but this would have to do.

## -7

HAT DOES NOT WORK." Sylas shook his head as he stared at RaeChaeline's sleek ride that was definitely not a police car.

"Oh, hush and get in," RaeChaeline said. He obliged.

There wasn't time for questions. She needed to leave before anyone caught on.

She drove away, gripping the wheel, thinking. She'd spent a long time meticulously considering her every word and action to maintain a certain image. And she'd equally been cautious on how she spoke about Gep.

Now, those skills would come in handy with the new gift Gep had given her: his heart. Pah! He could keep it if this was the cost. But she had to be cautious too in how or what this Sylas guy would say next.

"So," she tentatively said. "Spill. Who are you so concerned about that you keep visiting the morgue like it's your morning coffee?"

"I don't know if it's concern," he clarified. "Depends. How impossible of a story would you believe?"

This wasn't about her. It couldn't be about her. Sure, she may believe a few impossibilities—she's living proof—but she couldn't say it now. "Try me. You might be surprised."

Sylas propped his feet on the dashboard and rested his head on his hand. His feet swished up and down. "This girl," he began. "She may appear dead, but...she could be alive. Or, at least, be brought back to life."

RaeChaeline gave the guy credit. He knew something. She just wasn't sure what.

"This girl have a name? Or a reason for the miraculous?"

Sylas shrugged. "She works and doesn't work, the same as everyone else."

"Uh huh."

"She just..." He brushed his fingers through his hair absentmindedly. "I figure if the Trenchers won't check, I probably should. They'd want to know if there's a chance."

RaeChaeline squinted. "And the morgue would actually give that information to any ol' person who walks in and asks?"

"That's beside the point." He looked at RaeChaeline. "Ahh, I'm seeing a bit more now. There's something not working here."

She frowned. "Just talk about this Julia girl. Leave me out of it."

"Who said Julia? I didn't say Julia."

"You said the Trenchers," RaeChaeline insisted.

"Yes." Sylas moved his feet to the floor and sat up. "So you know them..."

"Better. I'm taking you to them. They can decide if you're a liability or just in over your head like the rest of us."

"Probably both."

RaeChaeline nodded. "Probably."

The car fell into silence, and Sylas began looking around the car again, like he was searching for something that wasn't there.

RaeChaeline sighed. "You can look all you want, just...keep your lips shut now. I mean this in the kindest way possible, but I can't risk you talking on this drive, mmk?"

Sylas smiled with his lips closed and pointed, demonstrating his agreement. Then he opened the glove compartment, pulled out the car manual, and flipped haphazardly through the pages, reading its functionality rather its words.

Minutes later, RaeChaeline pulled in to Dr. Evil's drive. "There's just one possible wrinkle we may run into."

"Okay," Sylas said.

"Uhmm." RaeChaeline pulled the car to the side and parked "Well, the wrinkle is, I don't know if they'll know I'm here. I'm not sure how this will work."

"If you show me," Sylas said. "I could tell you how it works, if you like."

"There's nothing to show. It's words."

"Oh, fascinating. I've found those rarely work as intended." Then, Sylas clarified: "That's not from me seeing how they work. Just my experience."

"That's been my experience as well."

They both climbed out of the car, and Sylas bounced on his tiptoes a few times as he looked around.

<h1 style="text-align:center">-6</h1>

NALIESE SET ASIDE HER…FEAR? HOPE? So often those two intermingled and disguised themselves as one another, so she wasn't sure. But she set it aside. She couldn't concern herself with Gep's missing body now. She had work to do.

She grasped a finger affectionately, like a toddler grasping their parent's. Except not like that. Her estranged sister—no, wait she was the estranged one. Her non-estranged sister was in literal pieces, and it was up to her to put her together, and if it didn't work then she had no one to blame but herself.

And everyone else waiting had no one else to blame, either. Nick would see the consequences, the true consequences of her monstrosity. Phoebe would forget, maybe, but Analiese couldn't look at her with what she knows, deep down, somewhere. Max was already on rocky territory with all the deception, and RaeChaeline and her never got on. Analiese had stopped caring about the Trenchers a long time ago; at least, she tried to, but that was more through distance than anything else, and with the close proximity…

And it all came back to Julia. It always came back to Julia.

So she picked up the finger, and began to mold it to the hand, then another and another. Each piece of the puzzle, the person, put together brought her closer to the moment where she'd realize her consequences had finally become fatal. Not from her... ability...only from her desperation, her very ordinary human desperation. It wasn't her exceptionality that could kill someone, not this time. It was her humanity.

She picked up the hair, the haphazard braid that Phoebe must have put together again, like last time. She wove the strands into Julia's scalp, smoothing each attachment with precision. She had to be exact. Attention to detail had always been critical as she crafted her skill. She considered herself an artist that way, and it would keep her from marring her...victims. But it wasn't marring this time, it was life at stake. And maybe putting her together perfectly was never an option, or never a solution, but the methodical attention to detail distanced herself from the repercussions, made it all seem less dramatic. It was just molding clay into a masterpiece. Even God waited to concern Himself with the breath of life until the frame was fully formed, so she could wait as well.

As she attached the last piece, the final pinky toe, she breathed a sigh of relief. She'd done all she could do. The rest was in the hands of whatever level of fate you believed in. She brushed her hair out of her forehead and slumped her head to the table, hands resting on either side. She waited, but nothing happened. She brushed her hand underneath Julia's nose, then touched her chest, and felt nothing.

Death. That's what it felt like.

She wondered about performing CPR, but wasn't sure if she was capable of that. And that's when she realized she'd need someone else. She had to face them, and soon, in case there was a timer on this sort of miracle curse situation.

She wanted to freeze. She'd tried flight and fight, and now all she wanted to do was freeze, but she had to choose to act.

Analiese took a deep breath and shook her head, then went to the door and opened it.

# -5

EMEMBER, CONTROL THE NARRATIVE. RaeChaeline led Sylas into the small clinic. A study, really, with a couple rooms for Dr. Evil's...experiments.

*Just where I left you*, she thought as she saw the crew assembled.

They were looking at Sylas. She cleared her throat and watched their gazes turn to her. Max jumped, and Mrs. Trencher put her hand to her chest.

"Hello everyone. Again." They saw her. That must mean... Her breath caught. Had she done it?

"Sylas!" Mr. Trencher said. "You must tell us if Julia can be fixed."

Sylas scrunched his nose and searched the room. "I don't know that I can do that."

But RaeChaeline couldn't get her hopes up. Not yet. "Great, you know each other." She didn't miss a beat. "Moving on. Max..."

Max jumped out of his seat. "I don't have a clue what's going on."

"Obviously. You care about that dead guy in the field?"

Mr. Trencher coughed. "Dead...? Guy...?" Mrs. Trencher clasped his arm.

"Dead guy in the field?" Dr. Evil appeared in the hall.

Max ignored him and responded to RaeChae. "According to the notes, it was more a volatile hot-and-cold, stuck-with-each-other-for-undisclosed-reasons situation."

RaeChaeline rolled her eyes. "Yeah yeah, you know the guy in the field more than anyone else and that's not saying much, I get it."

"In the field?" Dr. Evil repeated.

RaeChaeline turned to him and smiled a noticeably false grin. "He's not in your field anymore, not your problem."

Max took the opportunity to sit back down in his seat.

"Of course he's not in my field," Dr. Evil replied. "I told the cops they can search the premises."

RaeChaeline felt her face getting hot, and remembered he wouldn't see her anger if she didn't reveal it with her voice. "You let them?"

"We had the dead guy right here, of course I wasn't worried about some other dead guy."

Mr. And Mrs. Trencher stood in unison. "Other dead guy?"

"Sylas," Mrs. Trencher interjected, "Why don't you do your woo-woo thing to ease Mr. Trencher's mind, then us and Julia can head out."

"Perfect," Analiese appeared behind Dr. Evil, the picture of aloof composure. She would have learned that from Mrs. Trencher, except she had to learn that on her own. "I need someone to try CPR."

"Yes," Mrs. Trencher nodded. "CPR. Excuse us, won't you." The Trenchers followed Analiese back, with Sylas tentatively trailing behind.

Nick looked forlornly after them, but stayed.

RaeChaeline tapped her foot and pursed her lips. On the plus side, all this hubbub and not a single soul had muttered a word about her. "Soooo," she jumped back in. "Dr. Evil threw us to the wolves, who's surprised here."

"You could have told me I had another dead guy to worry about on my property!" Dr. Evil objected.

"Careful with your words," she warned. "Max. Dead guy, let's go."

Max looked at Nick, and Nick shrugged.

Max began to walk toward the door and opened his mouth, but RaeChae stopped him. "No talking. Just walk."

He frowned, but obliged.

NALIESE." MR. TRENCHER CLEARED HIS THROAT. "If you don't mind. What's this 'dead guy' thing?"

"Not to worry," Analiese said. "Either he's not dead or he's not here."

Mr. Trencher gulped.

"We don't want to know what she got Julia into." Mrs. Trencher walked up and touched her daughter's arm—Julia's, not Analiese's. "Sylas, make yourself useful."

He came forward. "As I tried to say earlier," he said, "I can't say if she can be fixed."

"Not that mumbo-jumbo," Mrs. Trencher said. "This is a medical situation. CPR. Obviously. Put that energy to use."

Analiese watched Sylas approach and put his ear to her chest.

Stillness.

His ordinary humanity could save Julia, while Analiese's ordinary humanity is what killed Julia. She wondered if this was what bitterness felt like.

He pressed on her chest to the rhythm of a song none of them could hear, and Analiese gulped.

Nothing.

He'd stopped, but Julia hadn't started. Just as she'd feared. Some things you can't come back from.

Analiese frowned. Sylas tapped the table, and that tapping was more than she could bear.

It should be the sound of Julia's heartbeat, but it wasn't. It was just a table and a man who had failed her.

She ducked out of the room before they could notice, and as she left the building hollered at Nick. "You coming or not?"

"Julia?" he asked.

She glared at him.

"Let's at least bring Phebe and plan some sort of...memorial or whatever..."

"That wasn't part of the deal."

"Deal's changed."

Analiese closed her eyes and breathed in, then out. "Things are about to get worse, Nick. Worse than that night. It's catching up to us, and you're in the crossfire. We need to go."

Nick looked at Phoebe, then back at Analiese. "Only if she comes."

Phoebe interjected. "I can stay. I'm okay. I'll be okay."

Analiese nodded, and Nick was hesitant. She wondered if he was remembering the last time he left people behind. What Analiese had done. How it all led to this. And while he paused, wondering whatever he was wondering, he did eventually follow. Analiese was thankful she could not read minds. She didn't want to know what he thought of her in this moment.

## -3

AECHAELINE DROVE SILENTLY, THINKING. To Max's credit, he hadn't said a word. He'd had firsthand experience that she would follow through on threats.

She needed Max to talk, but without talking about her or Gep. And she needed to know about...ack, Gep. The conundrum.

"I don't expect you to understand," she began. "But I'm going to ask you questions, and you're going to only give yes or no responses. Yes?"

Max side-eyed her. He had caught on that her lack of trust was an insult. "...yes."

She nodded. "Good."

Now, she just needed to be careful how she phrased things. She had to get it just right.

"Earlier I'd said that you wouldn't find me until Gep leaves the building. Did...that happen?"

Max's brow furrowed and his mouth opened a bit. He wanted to say more. He was about to. He had questions. But instead... "No."

"Hmm. Something is off." She tapped the steering wheel. "You

24

didn't find me. I came back. That's different. But wait!" She looked at him. He pointed at the road then turned her face forward. Still totally clear straight road. He was paranoid over nothing.

RaeChaeline cleared her throat and looked at him again. "Backseat driver even without words. Your ability to be a nuisance knows no bounds."

Max smiled proudly, ducked his head and outstretched his hand in a mock bow.

"As I was saying...I also said something about Analiese fixing Julia. That *did* happen."

No response. She looked his way again, very aware an oncoming car was nearby and a turn was upcoming. "Y-yes," he sputtered.

She looked back at the road in plenty of time. "So half of it did come true. But..." She wondered if a question would cause problems. She didn't think so. But she wasn't about to bank on that. "But the other part...no one...previously dead...walked out?"

"Mmhph..." Max really wanted to say more.

RaeChaeline sighed. "Okay, if you don't reference me or Gep at all, you can spill what you know. Did you see anyone or not?"

"I didn't see anyone, but Ge...dead people...? are in the back of the medical clinic. How would I know what happened?"

"How would you know?" RaeChaeline yelled in exasperation. "You were *there* and *someone* alluded to a *dead body* leaving the building you're at, and you didn't think to check?!"

"Why would I? It's a dead body."

RaeChaeline put her hand to her forehead and let out a huff. So, it didn't work. She'd have to try again. Something else.

"So uhh... Where are we going?" Max asked.

RaeChaeline gave a dry laugh. "If we're lucky, we're going to watch a dead body walk out of a building."

# -2

**T**HEY WERE PARKED ON THE STREET, and RaeChaeline was peering at a building further down. "We need binoculars."

Max laughed. "It's dark out. Binoculars aren't what ya need. Drive closer." He reached over the seat and grabbed the keys, and RaeChaeline lightly smacked his hand.

"Shush. We can't drive closer. I don't know where the property line begins and that might matter."

"Soooo are we stealing the corpse the cops took or something? This is because I puked and incriminated myself, isn't it."

"Well it's not because I got my fingerprints all over him getting you his ID."

He frowned.

"But it's not because of you puking, either. Don't you know you can't just puke around dead bodies in fields? Idiot."

"I'm not exactly comfortable harboring and poking around dead bodies like you."

She shrugged. "This one won't be dead anymore."

And right on schedule, Max saw a side door open and a figure step out—presumably a live one.

"What the…"

"It worked," RaeChaeline whispered. She moved the car out of park and creeped forward, headlights still turned off. Incognito ish. "You wanna reunite with this roommate?"

Max shivered. He didn't remember anything except the corpse. The sparse apartment. The room with the circus curtains, and the other room with notes of a volatile relationship of some sort. The worry that still lingered, that they might have been planning a kidnapping or hostage situation; he still wasn't sure, because he still had the darkness following him. And the warning, in his handwriting, that haunted him. *"Be afraid…Run."*

The figure, more of a silhouette at this point, walked toward the sidewalk, a bit unsteady. Probably shook up from just leaving a morgue and being dead for awhile and all.

RaeChaeline reached for the headlights, but Max put up his hand. "Wait."

"No?" she asked. "Wasn't this what you went through torture for? Your past life, your identity—it's right there for you."

Max shook his head. "My identity came with me and told me to leave the past behind."

RaeChaeline shrugged, flipped on the headlights, and sped past the figure and down the road. "Fine. I suppose we know where he lives if you ever change your mind."

Max nodded and smiled, then froze. "Wait."

"Don't tell me you changed your mind again."

"Where he lives. My notes! You have to take me there so I can clear the place before he arrives!"

RaeChaeline glared at him. "No second person sentences from you, remember!" Then, she rolled her eyes. "Consider me your chauffeur, I suppose, but you owe me."

"Turn here," Max instructed.

RaeChaeline sighed with the burden of being mandated something as mundane as directions. But she turned.

As she drove, she pursed her lips in thought. "Hmm, Fancy..."

"Fancy?" It came out of nowhere. She knew Analiese as Analiese, not Fancy.

"You called Analiese Fancy," she explained. "To protect her."

"To deceive me, you mean."

"To distance her actions from her identity."

Max frowned. "That's one way to interpret it."

RaeChaeline nodded slowly. She opened her mouth and paused, choosing her words carefully. "The OG Fancy had the right idea. But...you won't call her Fancy now."

"I'm still figuring out what I call her. I don't know."

RaeChaeline shook her head. "Not what I mean. I'm telling you. There's a...new Fancy. You call...someone else Fancy now."

"Huh?"

RaeChaeline groaned. "If I'm going to help you, there are stipulations. There are consequences to avoid. So... You have a new Fancy you're a sidekick to."

Max's face lit up. "Oh, you! You mean you!"

RaeChaeline's eyes widened, and she slammed on the brakes. "Sssshhhhhhh..." She frantically looked around like someone could hear. But only her and Max (and of course you fine readers) were privy to this conversation. "You can't... No second person references allowed. Ever. Just Fancy."

Max rubbed his forehead. "To distance y—...this new Fancy's... identity from her actions."

RaeChaeline added. "And...no introducing a certain someone as

Fancy. Never tie the name Fancy to...someone. It's gotta be clean and separate. You tracking?"

"Not really."

RaeChaeline sighed and started driving again. In a patronizing and exasperated tone she said, "So you're getting the papers with *Fancy*. There is no RaeChaeline, no second person. Fancy and Max are going to the apartment. That's it."

"Agh," Max said. "We passed our turn."

RaeChaeline slammed on the brakes and swerved. "You didn't tell me?"

"You're distracting."

"*Fancy!* Fancy is distracting."

Max nodded. "Right. Fancy. Not Analiese, a new Fancy, for the good of humanity or something."

"You're catching on."

"I can't reference a certain name that rhymes with Maybelline, and I can't even say..." He whispers, "...Y-O-U." Then back to normal volume: "Ever."

RaeChaeline rolled her eyes. "Not even in whispers."

"In reference to anyone? Or just...the new Fancy?"

"Fancy."

"...Fancy drives a hard bargain."

"Always has."

"Touché."

They didn't beat Ferguson home. He arrived while they were sorting out Rae—I mean—Fancy's identity. But don't fret. Max's memories will return to him in paper form or otherwise at some point in this story. You'll see...

# -1

THE FIRST THING JULIA HEARD WAS A SNIFFLE. Immediately after, she noticed the cold surface underneath her, much too cold. She moved her fingers gingerly and felt the edge of the table, though she didn't know it was a table at this point. All she knew was it was cold, and she was alive and didn't like cold.

She was alive.

That meant Geppetto forced Analiese to put her together again.

But she couldn't be alive. *That's the end,* he'd said. And yet, somehow she was.

But something was different. She furrowed her brows and squinted her eyes open.

By the looks of the room, she'd guess she was at that Dr. Evil's place because of another fever or complication.

She turned her head, then blinked.

It was the Trenchers. And Sylas.

Not what she'd expect.

She closed her eyes again. She tried to remember. And she remembered that they tried breaking the contracts. That they must have failed, and that Geppetto was angry. That no one must leave the tents and the end and then... Analiese had pushed her out of the tent. She had fallen to pieces, just as Geppetto had said. She was still under contract.

And then, she had ended up here somehow with the Trenchers. And...Sylas?

Even a clear mind couldn't put those pieces together.

She gave up on trying to remember, gripped the edge of the metal table, and pushed herself up.

"Julia," Mrs. Trencher gasped.

"I'm here," she said. "I'm...all together here."

"We should probably leave," Mr. Trencher said.

"Yes. Julia dear, you won't believe what you've put us through. There's this doctor here they call Dr. Evil, and they're talking about dead bodies, and this is just not the place for the Trencher household."

Julia put her fingers to her forehead and squinted. "I was a dead body though."

"Yes, but not like..." Mrs. Trencher trailed off. "Anyhow, the circus is gone, that silly excursion over, so we can all go back to the way things were."

"The way things were," Julia repeated.

"The way things were," Mr. Trencher agreed.

Sylas smiled. "The Dr. Evil nickname works pretty well, so I'm actually in agreement with you all. Unlikely alliance, huh?"

Mrs. Trencher frowned. "Not you."

"But the way things were," Julia repeated again and touched Mr. Trencher's arm. "I'm not the way things were."

"Whatever do you mean?" Mrs. Trencher said. "You're all fixed. We can go."

"Fixed." Julia hopped off the table. "Because of the contract. But he said... 'The end'..."

"Whatever are you going on about?" Mrs. Trencher said. "She must have hit her head."

"She was dead," Mr. Trencher mused. "It may take time."

"But I..." Julia felt her arms, her shoulders, then her face. "I'm fixed."

"Yes, we said that."

"No, not fixed like before. Fixed. 'That's the end of that.'"

Mr. and Mrs. Trencher looked at each other. Sylas stared at the floor quizzically.

"I... I fell apart because of a contract. And, part of the contract... Geppetto said whoever fell apart that it's 'the end of that.' I thought... I thought for sure that'd mean the end of me. But I wonder, since I'm here, maybe that's the end of breaking apart. Maybe I'm fixed more...permanently."

"Permanently?" Mrs. Trencher said.

"Circus tricks," Mr. Trencher added satisfactorily.

That got Sylas's attention. He looked up and studied Julia, eyes scanning her form, catching himself and studying her face, her eyes, her chin, her nose, her ears. Did she work differently than before? And could he see it if so? She wasn't sure.

Mrs. Trencher sniffed. "I wouldn't believe anything those tricksters have said, but I'll admit if true, at least something good came of all this."

"Good?" Julia asked.

"Of course."

Julia wrapped her arm across her stomach.

"What's wrong? Are you ill?"

Julia closed her eyes. Was she ill? Was something wrong? " I...I never asked to be fixed. I... I don't know if I'm ready. If I want it."

Mrs. Trencher laughed, and Sylas started.

"Of course you do," Mrs. Trencher said. "Don't be silly."

Sylas moved to the door and listened. "We should go."

"Yes!" Mrs. Trencher clapped. "Let's."

Sylas opened the door, and Mr. and Mrs. Trencher followed. Julia tentatively stepped forward. She didn't know what she wanted. This wasn't the story she'd signed up for. "Th-the circus," she said.

"It's gone," Mr. Trencher said. "We'll fill you in after we're safely home."

"Gone." Analiese, RaeChaeline, Phoebe,... Nick. They had been trapped. If they were gone...

Julia trailed behind them, not certain what was next. She'd never known how to decide between the Trenchers life and something different, but now that something different was... "Gone."

As she came to the main entry, though, a woman was sitting, waiting. Julia rushed to her, crouched and clasped her hands. "Phoebe!"

Phoebe looked at Julia and smiled tentatively.

"You don't remember me," Julia said. "I mean, not much."

"Geppetto's decision, and darkness, and..." she trailed off.

"Yes!" Julia could hardly contain the joy at this simple thing, that Phoebe was exactly who she knew her to be. "Do you know what happened to Nick? The circus?"

Phoebe thought, then shook her head. "I'm not sure. You were... dead. That's all. I'm relieved to see you well."

Mrs. Trencher cleared her throat, and Julia looked her way, then held up a finger.

"Phoebe, we're leaving," Julia said. She paused. She couldn't leave Phoebe behind, alone, with Dr. Evil. "We can find a place together. If you want."

Phoebe glanced down the hall, where Dr. Evil was approaching.

"Leaving so soon?" Dr. Evil said. "I should probably do a full examination..."

Julia stood. "I'm fully fixed. Nothing worth examining."

"Fascinating," Dr. Evil said.

Julia looked back at Phoebe. "Come with us, Phoebe."

Phoebe shook her head. "I should stay. Trust me."

Julia shivered. She didn't know if it was intuition, a vision, or something else, but even with her missing memories Phoebe always exuded confidence in her own decisions. Perhaps it was because she'd seen so many monumental decisions with every face she encountered, so she'd learned where each decision could lead. At any rate, Phoebe's decision now was to stay with this man the circus folk didn't trust. And Julia had to hope it was the right choice.

"I'll come back and check on you," Julia said. "I'll find out about the others, and then I'll come back for you."

Phoebe nodded and gave a soft smile. "I won't remember. But if I could, I'd look forward to it."

Julia stared at Dr. Evil. He grinned. "Come back any time."

Julia didn't know what the worry was. She could only imagine from Dr. Wise, but that could be completely different. Still, she had to try something. "Don't touch her," she vaguely warned.

Then they left.

"So, just you and me." Dr. Evil said to Phoebe. "What now?"

Mere moments after the Trenchers and Sylas left—escaped?—there was a rap on the door. Dr. Evil plastered on a smile, patted his hair just so, and opened the door.

"Hello fellows," he said to the officers. "How can I help you?"

Phoebe watched from her seat curiously.

"Sir, I'm sorry to bother you again," an officer said. "Do you know this man?" He held up a grotesque photo of a corpse's face, bloated and largely unidentifiable even if Dr. Evil knew him.

Dr. Evil grimaced just a bit for show and shook his head. "Can't say I do. What happened?"

"He was uhh... in your... that is to say... he was found when we were searching the circus grounds."

Dr. Evil put his hand on his chest. "No! So there was a casualty from the fire. I can't imagine. His family must be devastated."

"Well, we actually... It wasn't the fire. I mean, probably, the M.E. hasn't confirmed that yet. I mean..." The officer grew flustered and looked at his partner. "We're trying to identify him. And any witnesses or persons of interest."

"I'm sorry I can't help. If the vanished performers turn up, maybe. But..." He glanced at Phoebe. Her eyes were wide, and he willed her not to approach.

"Have you by chance..." The officer cleared his throat. "Have you by chance seen the body today? Or any suspicious characters?"

Dr. Evil frowned. Now he didn't know how to respond. "The body? I thought you... I haven't been to the morgue if that's what you're asking. It must have been someone else."

"That's not what... I mean to say... the body has been...stolen."

"Stolen? How nefarious."

"Yes, very. If you notice anything suspicious or come across anything, do please call."

"Absolutely! Feel free to search the grounds again for any leads. It's possible the individual would have been at the scene to tamper with evidence, too."

The officer smiled. "Oh yes, absolutely! We can only hope the attempts to cover up the crime ends up incriminating them instead. Thank you for your cooperation."

Dr. Evil smiled again, nodded, and closed the door. He looked at Phoebe. "That was close. You don't remember a dead body in the fields, do you?"

Phoebe pondered. "...Julia."

Dr. Evil shook his head. "Not her. Some man."

Phoebe shook her head.

"Well, let's hope they be on their way quickly."

Phoebe scrunched her nose, unconvinced.

He gestured down the hallway. "Now come, do help. If you're sticking around may as well be useful."

He began walking toward the back entrance, and Phoebe tentatively stood and followed. He opened the door and pointed at the ground to the side. "Let's get this back inside."

She approached the doorway and peered around the corner. Her face paled, and he laughed. "Had to help the prophecy along ya know, I'm not a patient man."

She knelt down and felt the man's pulse. He was cold, had been long dead. "The cops..."

He waved his hand. "They're not looking for him. At least, not yet. We must get him inside."

Phoebe looked around.

"You don't know who this will incriminate," Dr. Evil cautioned. "Trust me."

She rolled her eyes. "I'll never trust you." But she did acquiesce to his original request, and lifted Geppetto's corpse at the shoulders off the ground.

Dr. Evil grabbed Geppetto's legs and smiled. "That's all right. Trust isn't required."

*They started as classmates in university where many grand rivalries in stories begin.*

*Two sides of the same coin: One born in wealth and luxury, spoiled to believe he could have everything he wanted. The other born to believe he was too good for the life he was given. Both obsessive in their studies, ambitious, seeing everyone else as pawns in the story they were crafting.*

*Viel studied medicine, to build a better human. One in his own image, perhaps.*

*Gep studied psychology, to build a better human. One for his own image, perhaps.*

*Both delusional to believe they could control what they were messing with.*

*And as rivalries tend to, they both set their eyes on the same girl, too.*

*"She may fancy you, Gep. She may even fancy you over codgy old me. But when she's ready to settle, she'll see what's right for her."*

*"A cushy home doesn't win over love,"* Gep said. *"Haven't you read anything?"*

*"This isn't a fairy-tale, Gep. This is the real world, where love can be bought for the right price, and everyone else gets the scraps. You're gonna end up with scraps if you keep living with these fanciful notions."*

*Gep frowned. None of that tracked to him.*

*Viel laughed. "Ahh, Gep, what an absolute artist you are." He said "artist" with a condescending tone.*

*"A total dreamer,"* Gep replied in earnest. *"But just you wait. I'll find the right magic to make my millions and leave you in the dust."*

*Viel sniffed. "New money doesn't scare me. Besides, magic is a shot in the dark. Science is certain, the proven track to success."*

*But, science was not certain, Viel would soon learn. Magic wraps its claws around science, and science dips its toes into magic's force, volatile and inseparable beings. And so, when Viel had his breakthrough discovery, magic would not let it alone.*

# 0

STORIES ARE A MYSTERIOUS THING. They weave in and out, this way and that, they intermingle. They laugh at the linear, and twist and hop and dance their way through a dozen characters. They veer to the side when you least suspect.

This isn't Max's story, nor Julia's—in fact, no one individual can own a story. They simply play their part in one another's stories as they entangle.

So, buckle in for the ride. We'll be traveling months into the future and decades into the past, discovering new characters that have been creeping about far longer than you, dear reader.

Ladies and gents, distinguished guests, you've only just witnessed the setup. The real show is about to begin...

# SIX MONTHS LATER

# 1

THE MAN LOOMS ABOVE ME as he approaches from the shadows. "What happened?"

I can't make out his face in the dark; he's nothing more than a silhouette. But I know exactly who he is. "Your grand plan didn't work," I say.

"Our plan, Max."

"The point is it didn't. Sound familiar?"

"I figured." He looks down, unable to meet my eyes. "But I lost time. Lo...lots of time. I was covered in... well..."

"You were dead."

The man looks up again, right at me. His eyes pierce through the shadows, a glimmer of light. "You say that so nonchalantly. As if it's...possible."

Julia steps forward. I guess she's here, too. She chimes in. "I was dead, too. But here I am."

"And here you are," Nick adds, grabbing Julia's hand and smiling at the shadow man.

The man's brows furrow. "And Phoebe...? G-Geppetto...?"

"Geppetto hasn't come back like you," Julia says. "That we know of, at least."

The man's hands are growing sweaty, and he wipes them on his pant legs. I realize my hands are sweaty too, and wipe them as well.

Julia continues, softens her voice: "Phoebe is alive. She's no longer part of the circus."

"She got out?" His eyes light up.

"She's out," Nick confirms. "Wish granted. But things are rocky 'round here now; you shouldn't just be turning up from the dead and asking questions."

The man crosses his arms. "Excuse me? I'm sorry my life inconveniences you. Let me just keel right up again so you can get back to your show."

The other guy steps up, the one who'd just been chilling hearing about life and death and such nonsense with eyes wide. The scene is getting rather packed. He holds up his hands between Nick and Julia. "Hey now, let's all cool our jets. I'm sure it's nice to see him in working order—relatively speaking—whatever history is involved."

"Who's this guy?" the man says.

"Hi," the guy grins. "The name is Sylas. Pleasure to meet you."

The man grunts. "And what do you gotta do with this?"

The guy—Sylas—shrugs. "Just along for the ride."

"You're about three rides back. If Gep is gone, far as I see it, you're all welcome. Obliged to help. I just need to know what I missed while I was out and where Jasper is."

Jasper. That's me. The old me, anyhow. I open my mouth to remind him, but the sound catches in my throat.

Julia folds her arms across her chest. "Gep's words came true, and you died. The fire spread, and Gep and I died that night, too."

"And what changed that for us lucky two, and who's to say Gep isn't next?"

Julia shrugs. "He could be. No one knows how this works, remember."

"And Jasper?"

I try my voice again, but it's gone. I don't know how to talk about the past me with my past roommate. It's too weird, I guess. To explain that I've changed, that I'm not Jasper anymore.

"Haven't heard of a Jasper," Nick says.

I begin coughing, trying to find my voice again.

Of course. They don't know I'm Jasper. They hardly know me. I hardly know them. Brought together by unlikely circumstances.

But somewhere deep down, I know this man in front of me. Or he knows who I was, at least. He just doesn't know my face after Fancy had her way with it, I suppose. Separated by unlikely circumstances.

The man runs his hands through his hair and paces. "So did you awake in the morgue, too, months ago? You and I awaken and Gep didn't...?"

Julia looks at Nick. "...not exactly."

Nick jumps in. "Jules was at Dr. Evil's with Gep. Analiese and Sylas brought her back."

"Julia and Gep? What about me?"

It was Sylas's turn. "You didn't wanna be at Dr. Evil's, anyhow. His name is Dr. Evil, remember."

"Cut to the chase, Nick. Why was I at the morgue when your Gep and Jules weren't?"

Everyone's forgotten I'm here. I went from the key player in the conversation to a fly on the wall; I'm fading into the background with no one the wiser.

Nick looks at the floor and taps his foot. "You were kinda... left in the field. We got Gep and Jules to Dr. Evil's, hoping he'd help. And the cops found your body and took it to the morgue."

The man laughs and shakes his head. It was a mad laugh. "Great. Honesty. Considering the way you won't look at me, I take it this wasn't from memory troubles, either. Glad to see what a fantastic team we all make." He frowns, thinks, then says, "Jasper wouldn't have left me like that. Something must have happened."

I timidly raise my hand and step forward, a squeak gets out. I need to find my voice.

The man looks at me again, his piercing gaze sees through me and it clicks. "Jasper. You're here. You're with..." His face hardens. "You're with them."

I'm visible now, and I try to explain myself. I try to speak. But the words won't come.

The man steps forward, into the light; but his face is darkness, swirling darkness, with only the eyes piercing through like light. "Why would you leave me, Jasper? Why would you leave me to rot as if we were nothing?"

The man begins to wither and collapse in front of me. Now he's fading; he's dying again. Nick and Julia and Sylas step back in fear. "Why would you leave me to rot as if we were nothing?"

My eyes begin to water. I want to explain. I want to recognize this man and care for him again the way I must have once. I want to go back to that time, and at the same time I don't. I'm someone else now.

The man's skin and muscles and darkness fade to bones, until there's nothing but a skeleton reaching out to me. "Why..." it whispers.

Then I wake up. For the third time since he left the morgue, he haunts my sleep.

# CIRCUS OF STRANGE MARVELS RETURNS ON TOUR!

The Circus of Strange Marvels is back with fantastical performances, touring across the region and returning to the original site in the barley fields.

Analiese—"just Analiese," the new owner—invites folks far and wide to return for "a truly unique experience like nothing seen before. Like a phoenix from the ashes, the show is bigger and better than ever."

Aside from Analiese's reference to the flames, the performers and circus hands are curiously silent on the change in ownership and the scandalous rumors from the past.

It was just last year that Great Geppetto's Circus of Strange Marvels vanished in flames, amidst many fantastical rumors and the stolen corpse of a suspected homicide victim. No suspects or leads were found.

The John Doe case remains unsolved, and any tips or information can be sent to 1-800-CIRC-DOE.

# 2

O FFICER JENKINS' HANDS SHOOK and clenched the red and yellow flyer, the same one that caused so much trouble end of last year. Only now, at the top was added on "Bigger and Better" in blocky gold lettering. The name "Geppetto's" was crossed out with the same gold line, and at the bottom in smaller gold print it said "under new ownership."

The story had created unease at first. A dead body—a stolen dead body at that—with no leads. The community was in uproar wondering who was next and who would be brought to justice for this. But, no one was notably missing. No one missed the corpse who had disappeared. And so, the worry faded, the unease faded, and Officer Jenkins was able to put that unsolved mystery behind her. Until now.

Questions were coming.

Journalists would be coming out of the woodwork, followed closely by the town council and other concerned citizens pressuring her. She'd have to find a lead... well, yesterday... before she became a laughing stock again.

She pulled out the meager file, the sole documentation that *something* had happened, though no one was really sure what.

Not this time.

She would get ahead of it, meet the new owner of this pesky circus of criminals that had the nerve to call itself magical. She'd find answers.

# 3

JULIA APPROACHED THE CIRCUS with Sylas trailing behind. The Circus of Strange Marvels was different now than it had been then. And yet, it was the same, too. Each performers' banners were once again prominent as spectators approach the entrance, only Phoebe and RaeChaeline's banners were no longer there; others took their place alongside Nick. The red and yellow tents were there, but true to Analiese's word, "bigger and better." The historical wagons were moved to the center of the pathway, a relic of this circus's roots in more ways than one. Looking far back at circus history and referencing the past year's meager start.

Julia touched the tent's cloth, pondering. Sylas was drumming his hand on his leg and looking around. "It's working," Julia muttered to him.

"Sorta," he responded.

"Better than before."

"Just different than before." Sylas shrugged. "The same, I mean. But different."

"You read my mind."

"That's not how I work."

Julia pursed her lips. "...yeah, sure."

*The same, but different.*

Just like Julia. Julia hadn't broken apart since the fire. And yet, somehow she felt like she'd never recovered. She was still back there, in that moment, falling apart and no one had put her together. At least, not the way she was supposed to. Her body had changed, yet she herself hadn't caught up to it. She was stuck in a loop, and Analiese's circus was a representation of that.

She wondered if Sylas saw it all. She hadn't quite figured out what he saw.

"Julia!" Nick was peering out of the tent, smiling. "I was hoping you'd come."

"Analiese wouldn't want me here," she said.

Nick scoffed. "'Course she does. She wants to show off, you know that."

"She... She doesn't want to see me, though."

Nick shrugged. "I do."

Julia smiled. "I suppose that's all that matters."

Nick glanced at Sylas, then back to Julia. He gestured her inside. "Come see."

Julia and Sylas entered and looked around. It was the same tent. Lanterns in a circle.

And yet, it was different. Nick pointed up. Spotlights above instead of puppet strings. "New-fangled stuff."

"No strings," Julia said.

"Her contract's a bit more lenient. The lack of strings represents that, I suppose." Nick lightly brushed his fingers against Julia's.

"She's good to you?" Julia asked.

"She's...building a good place. For all of us."

Nick was admiring the space again and didn't notice Julia shake her head, but he looked her way when she moved her hand away from his. "Not me."

Julia wasn't one of the "us" after the fire. She wasn't quite ordinary, she never would be. But she couldn't belong to these people now, either. She was stuck in between. "Sometimes I wonder, would I have belonged? If I hadn't tried to break Gep's contracts? But wondering doesn't change things. This is the world I chose."

It was Nick's turn to shake his head. "You didn't choose this world. Gep doesn't get to win. Not anymore.

# 4

NALIESE STOOD OUTSIDE HER WAGON, her home. It fit like a glove, and she didn't know why she'd ditched it for the Trencher home. Or at least, she didn't want to think about why.

Now she was playing host to Julia, apparently. Julia was approaching the circus with Sylas, that man who had whisked her back to her life, the life she belonged in, so quickly. As it should be.

But it was Analiese's turn to show Julia what she could do, what home she could make when Geppetto wasn't around to mess it up.

Analiese squinted. Julia was smiling at Nick, who had popped out of his tent to greet her. That sweet, naive smile of a girl falling for a rascal. That's not part of the plan. That's not the story Analiese had signed up for.

It didn't faze her for long, though. She'd never gotten the story she would choose; why should now be any different?

Analiese walked down the steps of the wagon. She could approach Nick's tent. She could make sure to direct them all to the right story, the one they each belonged in. That's what she always does.

And yet, there was this gut feeling that she didn't get to make that call anymore. That she'd too boldly played her hand and lost, and that she didn't deserve to step back in.

But if this was the story she was dealt, she would have to make her home in it yet, one way or another.

# 5

PHOEBE KNEW SHE HAD MADE THIS CALL for a reason. That she'd stayed with this man—Dr. Evil—against others' better judgment. She always relied on her own intuition. Somehow, with the little memories she carried, she still knew that her own gut had gotten her here; that somewhere deep down, her subconscious knew and guided her. She needed to trust something in this world, and she trusted that gut instinct. Some might call it fickle feelings, but she thought of it as discernment, as a gift to complement her loss.

So she stayed with this Dr. Evil, fully knowing she was in harm's way but not remembering why, clinging to the certainty that she was needed here. For something. What, she wasn't sure. That would require a memory she didn't carry.

Each night she'd return to her circus wagon, say hi to Analiese and Nick, and each morning after her cup of coffee at Dinah's Diner she'd be drawn to Dr. Evil's lair again. It was a predictable routine, which was all she had. Her body knew where to be even when her mind didn't.

As cluttered as Dr. Evil's study habits were with papers and books strewn about, he was a stickler about dust. Phoebe would refuse most requests he made, so eventually he'd hand her a feather duster and get her cleaning the office top to bottom, knocking down the cobwebs that formed so quickly, and instructing her to leave the vermin alone. "We have a moral code about all forms of life around here, ya know," he'd insist. Not that Phoebe would remember that claim. She didn't even remember that she hadn't signed up for the job, wasn't his janitor, wasn't being paid for the task.

Besides the more menial tasks, Dr. Evil would request to run tests on her—bloodwork, brain scans—and each time she'd decline. He'd ask her questions, and sometimes she'd answer. Sometimes she refused because she didn't remember. Sometimes she refused because she knew it wasn't safe to divulge to this man. It didn't matter. He'd take whatever he could get. Sometimes she'd ask him questions, too, though she hadn't figured out yet what questions she was supposed to be asking. She just knew she needed to find something out.

Julia would visit her as promised, and Dr. Evil would make it a point to note that his treatment of Phoebe was impeccable, and that Julia was welcome to join them if she wished. She'd always refuse. And she didn't care what Dr. Evil said; she cared what Phoebe said. Phoebe would say she's happy, that she's where she's supposed to be, and Julia wouldn't understand. Couldn't understand. Julia had always wanted to know that she's where she's supposed to be, and just as she thought she'd figured it out, it'd been ripped away from her. Somehow Phoebe had found it here, in unlikely circumstances, and she truly meant it. Somehow.

But most of the time, Phoebe and Dr. Evil would study Geppetto's corpse. He'd propose things Phoebe wasn't sure were ethical, and Phoebe would sometimes oblige. He was trying to bring Geppetto back he said, and she believed him. Mostly.

And each visit she grew continually more and more fixated on the door to the attic. She didn't know that she was growing fixated over days and weeks and months. She didn't remember that each time she looked up or each time she asked Dr. Evil about it he'd distract her until she'd forget, pull her into another space for another thing. It was just a creaky looking wooden door in the ceiling of the hall, you'd pass right by without a glance.

But, if you chanced to look up, if you chanced to pay close enough attention to your surroundings and look away from the eerie rooms and toward the unassuming ceiling, you'd notice the outline. Worse, you'd see the lock bolting access to it from the outside world, and bolting access from it to the world outside. For which purpose, you couldn't be sure. As I mentioned, Dr. Evil didn't like to talk about it.

And with a glance away, the wondering would leave, the yearning would dissipate. Phoebe would forget what she had seen and carry on with her dusting, perfectly content once again in that feeling that she was meant to be here for reasons yet to be seen.

# 6

ENKINS APPROACHED THE TICKET BOOTH. "You know this man?" she held up a photo of John Doe.

The crew member frowned. "I wasn't involved in that last year; I'm new."

Jenkins smiled. "Well, at least ya know why I'm here."

He nodded. "You want Analiese, she's been around. Her right-hand man, too."

"Got a name?"

"Look, I'm just here for the gig. I don't want trouble. I don't know anyone 'cept Analiese since she pays me."

Jenkins nodded. "Fair enough. Where do I find Analiese?"

He pointed at the circus wagons.

"The creepy wagon?" she asked.

"Aren't they all?" he laughed. "The one with the monstrous couple dancing."

Officer Jenkins put her hand to her forehead to block out the sun. She saw the illustration of the beautiful woman dancing with the beastly figure, bold lines and streaks bringing unease to the wagon tableau. A woman stood outside the wagon, glaring at a group outside a nearby tent.

Jenkins approached. Not ideal to question someone in a bad mood, but that's par for the course, even in non-steal-a-corpse situations.

The woman named Analiese descended the stairs and began heading toward the tent. The group had disappeared, but probably into the tent itself rather than the magical presumed "vanishing" of last year.

Jenkins interrupted her. "Excuse me. Analiese."

Analiese turned toward her. She plastered on a smile and her entire demeanor transformed in an instant. "Hello, welcome. How can I help?"

Jenkins pivoted. "I understand you've been around since Geppetto days."

Analiese's smile froze, and she blinked. "I was a simple stagehand then. Haven't seen him since the fire."

"I was actually wondering if you recognize this man." Jenkins held up the photo again.

Analiese studied it carefully. "This is about that stolen corpse, isn't it?" She looked Jenkins in the face. "Don't remember him. Maybe he visited or something, but he wasn't with the circus."

"That's disappointing. Anyone else around I could ask by chance?"

"Sure, one of our acts. Follow me." Analiese began walking toward a tent—a different tent than she had been walking to previously. Jenkins looked back at the tent the group had been at and wondered what the disagreement was about. But, a year after a crime, it was more likely petty drama than anything worth pursuing.

She turned to follow Analiese to see where this path would lead. The easy path. More often than you'd expect, the easy path, the path you just happened across and travel down, ended up leading to the answer. And hopefully the path less traveled would be there to pursue another time, if it didn't vanish like the former circus or the corpse.

"Sully!" Analiese called out as they approached the tent, and out peeked a head. The man smiled when he saw Analiese, and stepped out. He had a large sticker on his shirt that said "Hello, my name is Sullivan."

Jenkins interjected before introductions could begin and shook his hand firmly. "Sullivan, pleasure to meet you. You must be Analiese's right-hand man."

Sullivan beamed at Analiese. "Happy to help where I can."

Analiese took a step back, letting Jenkins run with the discussion while she glanced back at the other tent.

"I understand you were here last year with Analiese as well," Jenkins said.

Sullivan ran his hand through his hair. "Sure, sure."

"Do you recognize this man? He was here the night of the fire."

Sullivan squinted at the photo. "Wasn't burned by the fire, though, it looks like. No, everyone survived that."

Jenkins nodded. "That's right, he was found nearby. You don't recognize him?"

Sullivan shook his head. "Sorry I can't help."

"Just one more question," Jenkins said. "Was Analiese gunning for Geppetto's job back then, too?"

Analiese jumped back in. "I see what you're getting at, but you've got the wrong tree you're barking up."

"Oh?" Jenkins asked. "Seems like you'd have quite a bit of motive, playing up the magic and scandal to run this place. Probably run it better than Geppetto, don't ya think?"

"I'm just making the most of the unfortunate circumstances that lost us our jobs and family." She looked down at her clasped fingers. "There is someone else you might want to check with, though."

"Oh?" Jenkins asked.

"Not here," Analiese clarified. "The old Trencher home."

"I spoke with the Trenchers back then, but it couldn't hurt to check back in."

"Not them," Analiese said. "They can't keep track of anything. Their old home. Another cantankerous couple lives there now. Guy who claimed to be an investigator—I never believed him—started snooping around after everything. Didn't show a badge or give a reason, real sketch like."

Jenkins furrowed her brow. That was new. Something new, after all this time. She breathed a sigh of relief. Now if this impersonator could incriminate himself before the press show up for the story, that'd be great.

# 7

HE MAN LEFT THE APARTMENT ALONE. He hadn't been alone in years. It wasn't natural.

But beyond that, being alone probably meant his companion was in trouble. Jasper would be lost, and only he could bring his memories back.

Not to mention Phoebe. He'd planned to free her, and something... something must have went wrong. Though he couldn't be sure *what*; he just knew *who:* Gep.

And so, he began walking to the last place he'd seen Jasper, the last place he'd seen Phoebe: the circus grounds. They had just reopened, and he hoped they would provide the clues he had not yet discovered.

It was not as he'd left it. That is, he hadn't remembered leaving it, but it wasn't as he last remembered.

Geppetto's name was no longer part of the circus. It was just The Circus of Strange Marvels now, and he had a flutter of hope. But that flutter quickly turned sour as he noticed Phoebe's banner missing.

He scanned the banners again. RaeChaeline's was also missing, but Nick's was still there. Nick was here. Nick would remember the pieces he couldn't, would be able to fill in the gaps; if he was willing, that is.

The man swallowed, breathed in deeply, then exhaled. Nick had to agree.

He began walking toward the tents, gripping his fists to hold on to the last strands of hope.

As he got closer, he noticed Analiese at a tent with some cop. Not knowing what had happened, what perhaps he had done, the man ducked into the nearest tent. Sure, chances are either Analiese or the cop (or worse, both) could know something he didn't, but it'd probably be something he'd want to avoid being caught for. And he'd rather chance it with Nick than with Analiese.

"Oh, that's quite interesting."

The man turned to see who was in the tent with him, and found Nick and Julia with some other guy. "Just who I'm looking for."

"We're closed," Julia said.

"What happened?"

"We'll open soon," Nick jumps in.

"I figured. But I mean what happened with the contracts, the fire?"

Nick tensed. "We're not talking to reporters."

"Reporters?" The man shuddered. "I'm not... I lost time, and... you don't remember me?"

"Should I?" Nick asked.

The man's brows furrowed. "Maybe give it a minute. The memory... should return..."

"What memory?"

The man thought, wondered how much to divulge. Wondered

if it's possible to jog their memory. "I was at the circus, and... and then, I was leaving the morgue. I lost time."

"He's the stolen corpse," the guy who was hanging back said.

Nick and Julia looked back at him.

"What? It makes as much sense as anything else in this story."

Julia and Nick exchanged a look, and he knew. Whatever had happened to their memory, this was new. He couldn't wait around for this to change. This was new territory, like everything in his life as of late. "...corpse?"

"Maybe." Nick shrugged. "Dead in the field, found after the fire."

Julia added: "I died, too. But I'm back, so maybe... maybe somehow you are, too."

"What happened to Phoebe, G-Geppetto, Jasper?"

This time Julia spoke. "Phoebe and Gep aren't with the circus anymore."

She was free. Somehow, he didn't know how, but he'd done it or they'd done it. Whatever happened, Phoebe being free was what mattered. "Jasper?" He hoped at least he could get one answer, this answer.

"I don't know a Jasper," Julia said.

"Me either," Nick added.

Nick looked back at the other guy, who shook his head. "I'm just along for the ride."

The man thought, then said, "Well, guess I got what I came for."

"One more thing," Julia said. The man sighed and looked at her. "You're considered a stolen corpse since you went missing from the morgue. That may make things...interesting."

"Thank you," he whispered. He wasn't sure he was grateful for what he now knew, though, or what they did not know. And he not for the first time regretted that his memory would stay intact when he left while everyone else's would unravel.

# 8

RUE TO ANALIESE'S WORD, back at the old Trencher home there were still two characters going by names that didn't fully belong to them.

Max was still going by Max, and still the same Max you might remember. He still didn't connect with the name Jasper.

But Fancy was a borrowed name, not the Fancy you remember from before. Analiese had ditched the name when she ditched Max for Nick and kicked off this new circus thing. And right on schedule, RaeChaeline had picked it up, the next circus performer that needed to hide her identity.

So, when Jenkins knocked on the door, Max and the new Fancy startled. They never had company.

"What do we do with that?" Max asked.

"Answer the door, obviously," RaeChaeline said.

(The Max-and-Fancy banter you've come to know and love hasn't changed.)

Max drummed his fingers on the table. "No, I mean... This is good practice."

"Oh. Oh!" RaeChaeline snapped her fingers. "Dangerous, though. I'm on the spot."

"On the spot is when *Fancy* really needs things to work."

"Fine, fine. Uhh..." RaeChaeline groaned. "When I open the door..."

"Don't be too ambitious here."

"...I know."

"Okay."

"...When I open the door, the person on the other side won't reference me at all."

Max laughed. "Could have at least tried for a pizza delivery."

"Trying to protect this whole setup."

She opened the door. It was a police officer.

"You're right, should have tried for pizza," RaeChaeline muttered. Then out loud: "Hi!"

"Oh. Hi."

"Everything okay?"

"Sorry, I'm Officer Jenkins. Just...not what I expected." Jenkins peered behind RaeChaeline and looked at Max.

"Here for him?" RaeChaeline asked. "I'll let you two chat."

Max's eyebrows raised. It had worked. At least, so far. He gave RaeChaeline a thumbs up, then stepped in front. "How can I help?"

"I understand you're an...investigator?"

Max's stomach did a flip. Was he about to be arrested for impersonating? He wasn't sure. Was that a crime? Again, he wasn't sure. He swallowed. "I uhhhh, have done some private investigating, yes."

"Looking to hire a consultant?" RaeChaeline called out from behind.

Max was pretty sure she was supposed to stay out of this, but he appreciated the backup.

Jenkins smiled. "I understand you were hired by someone to investigate the circus last year."

"Err, yes...I mean, maybe. I can't speak to that. Investigator-client privilege thing ya know."

Max looked back at RaeChaeline, who was covering her face with her hand. "Smooth," she mouthed.

Max turned back to Officer Jenkins.

"So, that would be a yes."

"A maybe."

"Do you recognize this man?" She held up a photo, and Max's stomach flipped. It was the body from the field, the body that had risen again and walked out of the morgue, but this cop wouldn't know that. She'd just know that a dead body went missing, and probably the only evidence left was this photo and some vomit he'd left at the scene of the crime. Is vomit identifiable? He couldn't ask that. Too incriminating. But he couldn't deny seeing the body either, just in case.

"That's the dead guy that was discovered then disappeared, right?"

"Stolen, you mean."

"Listen, I got nothing helpful to add here. If I was looking into things at that time—which I can't divulge—it certainly didn't turn up anything." She'd keep coming back if she thought he'd have anything useful, and just claiming he didn't was more suspicious, not less. So he added, "Tell ya what, it sounds like you're not wanting to hire me, and if you're not a potential client I can let ya in on a secret."

"Oh?" Jenkins looked skeptical.

"Yeah. I... It turns out I'm not a good investigator."

"No kidding."

"I gave it a whirl, but I ended up deciding either no one had any info or they wouldn't divulge it to me. And I wasn't clever enough to get it out of them. So as much as I'd like to have something I could tell you, I don't."

Jenkins smiled. "Well I'm glad you would like to have something to help, at least."

Max smiled back. "Absolutely."

"I'm gonna need all your notes."

"Notes?"

"From your investigation," Jenkins said. "You may not be clever enough to put the pieces together, but I'm banking on you being better at record keeping than detective work."

Max swallowed. "Uhh... No?"

RaeChaeline swooped in. "I don't see a subpoena. In the meantime, it's Max's responsibility to keep his clients' records confidential. You understand."

Jenkins stepped back. "It'll be a search warrant. I'll be back."

RaeChaeline closed the door and sighed. "*Fancy* did not factor in your ineptitude under pressure when choosing words earlier."

Max looked at her. "Does *Fancy* have any ideas to get out of this?"

"First, burn your notes. Second, because you won't burn your notes even though Fancy told you to, hope a search warrant doesn't come through. And third, we need that living corpse."

# 9

O YA SEE ANYTHING?"

RaeChaeline clears her throat and gives me the side eye without removing the binoculars from in front of her.

"I mean... Does Fancy see anything?" I amend my statement. "But it's a question, I'm not sure it matters."

"It always matters." She looks back through the binoculars and adjusts the focus. "But no. Blinds are closed."

RaeChaeline hands me the binoculars, and I look through anyhow. I need to see for myself. Or, in this case, need to *not see* for myself. She's right; nothing to see here, folks. I sigh and set the binoculars between us in the car console. "So, what now?"

"Now, we wait."

"How come Fancy gets to say things in first person, but I can't say things in second person?"

"Fancy has to live with the consequences, Fancy can decide how to reference herself."

"One day Fancy will have to trust me."

"Did the OG Fancy ever trust you?"

I scowl. "That's beside the point."

RaeChaeline picks up the binoculars and checks again. Still nothing. She sets them down again.

"So, waiting. One of the things I least liked as an investigator."

"And yet here you are, still waiting to learn about your own life."

Max shrugs. "It's not my life anymore. Jasper said to leave it behind, and if I can't trust my notes, I can't trust anything."

"See, ya didn't burn your notes, did you?"

I don't answer.

"This is why steps two and three exist."

"Thank Fancy for her contribution."

"Mmhmm."

I jolt awake when RaeChae's hand bumps my chest.

"He's here!" she says. "He's going in!"

I blink and lean forward, peering out the dash. Ferg is approaching his apartment—our apartment? Did it still count as ours?

"What now?" I ask.

"Now, you and Fancy go say hi."

"Hi?"

RaeChaeline nods.

I wish she'd divulged her plan earlier to save the time. "I ca-"

"You can't, yeah, yeah. Thus says Jasper. Jasper got you into this mess in the first place."

"It's complicated."

RaeChaeline rolls her eyes.

"This guy knows me as someone else."

"He knows you. That's you! *You* just don't know you. He does!"

I go silent, cross my arms.

"It'll get you the notes you didn't get in time earlier..."

That perks me up. For a moment. Then I think some more, slouch and grunt my disapproval.

"If the cops find that, they can trace the handwriting back to you and that's just one more piece of incriminating evidence against you."

I frown, but don't budge.

RaeChaeline sighs and rolls her eyes again, but drives away. "Fine. It's a good thing Fancy came up with a step four."

# 10

OW IS HE?" RAECHAELINE PUSHED past Dr. Evil into the study. She hardly paused until Dr. Evil responded.

"As dead as ever, but I have a new theory."

Dr. Evil started searching through piles of books and papers. He didn't keep all his records neat. He sprawled things across his desk and study and every nook and cranny available to him. He'd ruffle through one book, dog-ear it, leave a coffee stain in another, then jump to a new one just to toss it on the floor like a tent that may or may not have saved his exact spot. He reserved being meticulous for things that really mattered, like his patients or his rivalry with Geppetto, or—in this case since it's one and the same—both.

Phoebe entered and nodded her head at the visitor. "RaeChaeline, good to see you."

"It's been a long time," RaeChae said. "Though you wouldn't know that, I suppose."

"But you do."

"No need to use your woo-woo on me. We weren't ever close, and I'm just here for Gep. No offense."

Phoebe smiled softly. "Of course."

"Stop chatting and start looking," Dr. Evil interjected. "Phoebe, my notes!"

Having few memories, Phoebe wouldn't recall where he set anything, but she jumped in and started searching, too.

RaeChaeline grew tired of waiting and rushed through the hallway and into the freezer with Dr. Evil close behind. She didn't know to look up, and she wouldn't have cared if she did. She had one focus: Geppetto.

RaeChaeline rested her hand on Gep's. "Some doctor you are."

"Same as all the others. Don't know how to bring folks back to life yet, besides your words that you *won't use*. Seems his staying dead is your fault and his life is in your hands."

She shook her head. "Too volatile. Speaking of, you know not to use second person with me. It's no wonder I don't venture out."

Dr. Evil harrumphed.

Meanwhile, in the study, Phoebe continued to search for she knew not what. She piled anything resembling "notes" in a pile for Dr. Evil to peruse. Until, sandwiched between a few papers strewn across an end table, Phoebe found a solitary key. She only thought about it a moment before pocketing it. She wasn't sure if she'd remember. She wasn't sure if it belonged to what she was looking for. How could she? She just knew it mattered.

She grabbed the pile of notes she'd found and walked back to the freezer where Dr. Evil and RaeChaeline were.

"Did you find it?" Dr. Evil asked.

She handed him the pile. He glanced at it with a frown, then with a harrumph, he tossed it to the nearest countertop, a few pages falling to the floor in his haste.

Phoebe approached Geppetto. "Gep is the same as...well, he's still dead for however long that's been. I'm sure you understand."

RaeChaeline smirked. "It's been months, Phoebe. It's been too long. But I've been painstakingly working on a solution since this guy's worth nothing." She gestured at Dr. Evil.

"I'm flattered," he piped in. "You flatter me. I pay for your circus, hide your murders, provide a medical clinic for you and all your lost pets, yet I'm 'worth nothing.'"

"Always have been. But keep trying and maybe you'll amount to something one day."

RaeChaeline touched Gep's forehead, as if he was feverish, leaned down and whispered in his ear. "I'll be back."

Then, she stood straight and waved at Dr. Evil and Phebe. "In the meantime, I've got another murder to cover up."

*The fairest in the land was arguably who Gep and Viel competed over. She had enormous sway on this story's origins, but merely as an object, an idea, an aspiration, and not as a human. She was too busy living her own story while they imagined her a prize in theirs.*

*But there was perhaps what you may call a second-fairest in the land. She wouldn't settle for scraps, and she wouldn't settle for being a mere prize. She very much matters to this story. She stood by as Gep and Viel ogled, she supported Gep in his experiments and plans to win the lady and his ridiculous competition with Viel. She considered herself twice as clever as either of them, but that didn't matter. She dreamed alongside Gep, and they supported each other. Where his support ended with words of encouragement, her support of his went the distance.*

*She would spend wee hours of the night researching to give Gep the edge he needed. Riches and fame and glory would come if they just pinpointed the parameters before Viel. If they just tapped into humanity's personality, uniqueness, and amped the volume up a notch. Superhumans, you could say. The next frontier of mankind. It was an outlandish notion, but what scientific advancement isn't?*

*Obsession. Gep and Viel knew about it, but RaeChaeline did, too. She didn't obsess over the science, the possibilities themselves. Those were fine, don't get me wrong, but they were meaningless to her. Whether the world remained the same or not, it was all the same cycle of history repeating itself, utterly boring. Some would find it fascinating, but not her. Instead of obsessing over how every human ticks, she obsessed over just one: Gep. What excited him excited her, not because it in itself was exciting, but because seeing his face light up was enough.*

*And so, when she had thought she'd discovered it... yes, it... what they'd been looking for all this time, she didn't gather them all together and announce it. She pulled Gep to the side. She whispered in his ear, and he lit up. Sure, he was hoping this would be the advancement that would land him the other woman. That was fine; RaeChaeline wasn't looking for that. She just was looking for a companion with a sparkle in his eye, and that she had. They were going to race ahead of Viel with him none the wiser, push him out of the discovery and let Gep ride off into the sunset with his bride, and with RaeChaeline to thank for it.*

# 11

AM ALMOST AS FIDGETY as when I went to visit Nicholas Cirque, or when I got tortured by Rae—I mean, by the new Fancy. (I don't know if this Fancy is as worried about how I refer to her in writing as to how I refer to her out loud, but I'd rather not find out considering what we've all seen she can do to make sure I never write about her in any form again.)

She'd instructed me to enter a police station. Without her because she's still laying low. (She trusts me not to screw this up more than she trusts her presence to not screw it up...maybe? Maybe I can take that as a compliment...?) The same police station that had someone showing up at our door today trying to trip us up in our words. (On second thought... why in the world is she trusting me with this level of responsibility?)

But I enter. I stick to the plan. And I hope it gets us out of this mess.

"Hi, uhmm..." I don't know how to say this without sounding sketch.

I remember Fancy's words. She'd given me the script and had me recite it five times to prove I had it down word for word. And just to be extra certain, she specified: "Don't you dare say 'stolen' in there. We don't need to reinforce that plausible and inaccurate storyline."

So I say, "I have information on the...circus corpse that may be of use."

The receptionist is pulling out a notebook. "And what's your...?"

I don't wait, though. Fancy was very clear I need to get in and get out without divulging more than she's permitted. She's waiting right outside to speed off for a quick getaway, and I gotta get the two details out first. "I believe his identification is Ferguson Tibble, and I believe I saw him entering an apartment complex...alive."

"Hold on a moment, sir." He's waving someone over while jotting as quickly as he can. But I can't stick around.

I spit out the address, the last crucial piece of information to end this homicide investigation. I see that Jenkins character approaching right as I turn tail, and I hope she doesn't recognize me. But it can't be helped at this point. I'm in the car and speeding away before anyone can give chase.

As we make our escape, I decide to chance it. "All right, we...I mean, Fancy and I...need the cards in our favor on this one."

Fancy frowns. "Why does Fancy feel like you're about to ask for something she won't give?"

"Fancy just put the entirety of step four in my hands. Does that sound like a safe bet to y...anyone?"

"Just what are you getting at?"

"This is what all the practice has been for."

Fancy rolled her eyes. "So short-sighted, pal. Practice isn't to get us out of a little scrape with the law. Practice isn't for reacting.

Reacting is too volatile, too emotional. Practice is for laser focus on the future, on our goals and dreams; whatever we want, we can make happen. But not if we..." She pauses for effect. "Simply. React."

I slump in my seat and mutter, "It's my dream not to be in prison for something I never did."

"And reacting would be trying to prevent it. Proactive would be getting you out after the fact with a comprehensive foolproof plan your Fancy puts time and thought into." She smiles satisfactorily.

"That's not exactly comforting."

Fancy shrugs. "Just saying."

I consider the worst options. I consider if I'm the type to break someone's trust. And I don't know because my memories are so new. I guess I just get to decide if I'm that type. I wish it wasn't a decision. I wish I knew and could be that person.

The paths split out before me in my mind—one where I fully relied on my own abilities to get me out of this mess, where the chances of landing in prison for nonexistent crimes seemed high, and where maybe, just maybe, she'd see fit to visit and help me escape if I wasn't just a scapegoat for her all this time. The other where I relied on Fancy's abilities, her cleverness, her "gift" that she considers a curse, and I betray everything we've been working all these months for, but I live outside of prison to see another day and make it up to her. I think. And I know which of those two guys I'd rather be. Right?

I have trust issues. We established that. I'd rather break someone's trust and earn it back than try to trust them. And in my defense, this is the lady who tortured me mere months ago and murdered the last bff she was dreaming with.

So...I do it.

I open my mouth and squeak out, "You have to..."

She swerves across the road then back again, and I grab onto the door. She slams on the brakes.

"...say words that..."

She puts the car into park, halfway onto the shoulder, and reaches across the seat, but I lean away.

"...get us off of..."

She unbuckles her seatbelt and clambers over until she's on top of me, and she's shoving her hands over my mouth to keep me from talking.

"...mmph mm hmph mhmph." I don't think that counts as words for this thing she does or is or has, but it's all I can do.

I remember Fancy's—the other Fancy, I mean—grasp on my mouth, how it had reshaped my face. I'm grateful that isn't this Fancy's thing. But it still hurts. And I missed my chance.

"Fancy!" she spits. "She doesn't have to do or say anything she doesn't want to."

She sighs and slumps forward when I stop fighting. Her head is halfway on my shoulder, and I know she regrets trusting me. She opens the side console, still leaving one hand firmly over my mouth, though I think I could fight it off, and I wonder if I should risk it.

She pulls a bulky gray object out, and I realize it's tape. I'm perturbed she had that so handy, but it's somehow fitting.

I twist my head to the side and clamp my teeth down on her hand. She howls and knocks me upside the head with the tape, not that it'd do any real damage.

Still, she's on top of me and that doesn't leave much room for escape in this cramped space. So, I open the door and lean to the side.

She falls off my lap and out, but I catch, and I remember. I'm still strapped in.

She's breathing heavily on the ground and glowering at me.

"You have to say something to get us off the cops' radar." I feel like I'm playing the children's red light game, trying to get the words out fast enough to catch the competition moving. Only this time, I'm trying to catch the competition before they move.

"Guess that's what I get, forgetting not to get in a tussle with someone less than half my age." She pushes herself to her feet, brushes her hair back, and is the picture of poise once again. She sighs. "So that's what you'll trade a friend for."

She glides around the car and gets back in the driver's seat.

"I'm not that young," I huff. She's got, what, a decade on me, but we both know that decade comes with a lifetime of cunning. But it doesn't matter. She has to do what I stated with no way around it, if I'm to believe her stories.

She's deep in thought, and I wonder if I should run. But eventually she says, "Officer Jenkins will see and recognize the man called Ferguson Tibble alive when..." It wasn't bound to come true quite yet, not without the last key piece.

I breathe a sigh of relief. She's saving me. Jenkins will see Ferguson and close the case thanks to...Fancy's...words as soon as she finds the trigger point.

And finally, she finds a way to end the sentence. "...when I have the man who's been riding in the car with me tied up in the Trencher's old home."

My heart rate picks up, and I look at her. She smiles. Always one to outwit me, to outwit everyone, I'd bet.

"Ready to go home, darling? Or would you prefer Jenkins never sees Fergie alive to exonerate you? How much are you willing to bet on me now?"

# 12

FFICER JENKINS LOOKED AT the apartment door, doubtful. But it was a lead, a diversion, a *something* that would clue her in to what someone was hiding in this case. Right?

Supposedly, she'd knock and a corpse would answer. But this wasn't a zombie show. It may be someone impersonating a corpse, but then she'd just find who they're covering for. She'd dig until she found an answer.

She squeezed her fists together, then shook them out. This was just a typical house call, she tried to reassure herself. But she knew it wasn't. It was anything from typical. It was the oddest cold case the town had seen and an unconventional anonymous tip.

Still, she needed answers, so she rapped on the door.

The door creaked open a crack, and a man peered out. She only saw his eyes and a scrap of hair. Sure, this could pass for the corpse, she supposed.

"I'm looking for a...Ferguson?" she said.

"What for?"

She wasn't sure if or how she should play her cards. She hadn't exactly been trained on how to ask a guy if he was dead earlier, or rather, how to handle a false claim that this man had been dead earlier. "Uh..."

His brows furrowed. "Did ya...forget?"

She smiled, forced a laugh. "No, 'course not."

The man sighed.

"Just a...wellness check," she landed on.

"I'm just swell." He rested his head on the door jam, revealing a smile through the small opening. "Who's asking?"

She didn't answer. Instead she decided to press a bit more. "You look familiar. Were you at the circus awhile back, before this new opening, I mean?"

He scowled, and this time he opened the door wide. He was tall and burly and intimidating, but more importantly she noted that his size lined up pretty well with that corpse's. "Don't play with me," he said.

"I'm not playing..." she stumbled. She studied his face. It could pass for a corpse probably, although this one wasn't dead or bloated or stiff or...dead. He wasn't dead.

"I do not look familiar. Let's be real."

She nodded.

"Did Jasper send you?"

"Who's Jasper?" she asked, taking a mental note to look into that name later.

"If Jasper didn't, then who sent you?"

"I-I-I don't know," she said. "It was anonymous. I just was looking into it. Sorry to bother you." She frowned, he frowned, then she left. She was baffled by the encounter, and she whipped out her notebook, wrote "Who's Jasper?" and underlined the name three times.

Unfortunately, that's all the notes she took before driving back to her office, her memories of the meeting dissipating with the distance. She wouldn't recall a Ferguson, or his questions, or the face that could belong to a living corpse if that anonymous tip was to be believed. She'd only have two words. She'd only have what she'd written down.

# 13

 SHUT UP AND SLOUCH in my seat and let Fancy drive me "home." Fancy follows me through the door into the old Trencher house, like guiding a lamb to slaughter.

She pauses in the entryway. I look back.

She's turned to the side, smiling into the large mirror above the curio. It's a plastered smile, the fake smile a woman on display gives. It's supposed to take your guard down, but to me it's just bared teeth, pretending to be nice before they bite.

I glance next to her reflection, at my own. Jasper looks back. He shakes his head. Disappointed. I blink the vision away.

I know this is my only—and I mean only—chance to escape Fancy's capture. Last time she had me tied up, she'd diced me to smithereens and played mind games I'd really not like to revisit.

She pats her hair with her fingers, just so, primping to ensure her pristine facade stays intact.

I consider using my knowledge against her. Saying something again about her letting me free. About her not hurting me, even trusting me again after all this.

She turns away from the mirror, gestures in the direction of the dining room. I frown and head that direction.

She's proven that she can one-up me in an instant. That anything I say can and will be used against me. So, I resign myself to the situation and let her tape my wrists behind my back then tape my ankles to the chair legs.

Next she'll tape my mouth shut, and that's when I realize I don't like this whole keep quiet plan. This is my only shot.

"Look, I know I crossed a line." I try to explain myself, but I know it falls flat. "I just... I won't survive prison. You know I'm not tough enough to make it in there. You would be. Clearly."

Her hand is bandaged now from my bite, and her vulturous eyes look down on me. You'd think she thought I had rabies or something. I'm not aware of a scalpel around, but I feel like she won't need one. I used my teeth out of desperation—what fanciful, imaginative ways could she come up with to hurt me using nothing more than her petite frame?

"I was scared. And desperate. I don't think as clearly and conniving as you. I..." I realize I can quote her, try to play to her ego a bit. Though I doubt it'll work, it's worth a shot. "I react. I react instead of thinking long term like you. Can't you find that a bit endearing or pitiable at least?"

She harrumphs and tosses the tape into the air, then catches it again nonchalantly.

"Look, you killed Gep..."

Her eyes shoot darts at me that could kill, but I gotta finish. I don't take hints.

"...because long term you saw it's the only way for him and you to realize your dreams. You think that strategically, that long term, you're that committed to your vision. So you're okay with me going to prison for awhile. That doesn't mean I am. All I got is right now, and the little morsel of my life I remember, and I'd like to keep that morsel of life out of prison. You probably can't understand that, but you can at least sympathize...? Maybe?"

She approaches ever so slowly, tiny step by tiny step. "Don't ever talk about Gep, and don't you ever talk about what I did or what I will do." A piece of tape screeches off the roll, and she rips it off. "Most importantly, don't refer to me in second person." Then she mashes it over my mouth. Trust issues.

# 14

OFFICER JENKINS BEGAN DRIVING TO THE STATION only to realize she didn't recall what had happened while she was out. She remembered driving to the mysterious address with a supposed dead guy, even approaching the door. She wracked her brain, and when it came up empty, she swerved into a last-minute turn and parked in front of the old Trencher house instead. Waiting. Thinking.

Something was up.

Jenkins sat in her car and tapped her finger on her notebook, as if touching the words enough would make them mean something. But her memory was black. Nothing to see here. Nothing to remember here. As if she hadn't written it, this thing in her very own handwriting that only she could have written. Not as if nothing had happened, but as if whatever had happened had gone dark.

The mysterious case had only gotten more so, as clues appeared and disappeared around her, and she couldn't make sense of what remained.

A private investigator who was horrible at investigating. A circus that disappeared and reappeared under new management. A rich doctor who housed the circus on his vast property. An address that supposedly had a living corpse inside. And a name she'd written on a page—Jasper—with no recollection of it. So many suspicious characters with no real leads.

It's no wonder this case had gone cold. There wasn't proof of a murder when the body wasn't there, no one was reporting a loved one missing, and it was just a claim of a dead body that the next day vanished. Nothing to investigate here. So when real proof of real cases piled up, naturally this would be the case to fall to the wayside. And it was about to happen again. It'd be a huge kerfuffle with the circus opening, press about mismanagement of a case and its victims. And then it'd die out on that note; no resolution, no explanation, just a new, ordinary case to read about predictable criminals and motives and evidence that didn't vanish.

Unless she did something about it. Unless she solved it soon before the world moves on.

If Max were around, he'd tell Jenkins to write everything down. (Only he wouldn't, because he didn't want her to keep snooping, but if he was on her side, I mean.) He'd learned that with this magic, the written word is the only thing that remains.

But Jenkins just knew to show up and look. Jot a few notes, sure. But not every detail. So she thought of where she should show up next, where she should press for information.

She could visit the circus (again) to find clues (again). If she kept looking, something new had to turn up at some point. She could visit the morgue. She could visit the Trenchers who mysteriously floated on the outskirts of all that occurred, with their daughter who fell to pieces and lived to tell the tale—at least, so the extravagant rumor with (once again) no proof goes.

Yet while Jenkins may not write every detail down, she wasn't without her ways. What intrigued her most was that there may be a firsthand accounting without the I'm-talking-to-a-cop-now, under-investigation filter. Just an accounting of what occurred as it occurred, hers for the taking. The private investigator's notes. She looked out her window and across the street at the unassuming home. She just needed the little extra nudge to make the search warrant a slam dunk. With nothing definitive pointing a specific way that would indicate this investigator's notes were relevant, it'd be a hard sell. She had to make them relevant. She didn't need the whole story. Not yet. Just enough to get the whole story. Just one little domino to find out what this circus was hiding.

# 15

J ULIA WALKED THE HALLS of the new house that she was supposed to call home. She looked out at the grand statue that was supposed to represent her, the prodigal who had fallen to pieces then been patched together again. And yet, the sculpture looked out at the world beckoning, and it saw hope. Julia no longer looked out and saw hope. She looked inward and wondered who she'd become.

The world had seemed so clear before. It told her she didn't belong here. It suggested she belonged out there, somewhere, with people like her. And she'd even found those people. But now, they carried on without her. She wasn't one of them anymore, never could be.

Nick claimed she'd always be one of them. But that's just like Nick to say that, it didn't count. Mr. and Mrs. Trencher pretended she was who she was always supposed to be now, that all was right with the world if they ignored what had been.

Nick was the opposite. He pretended nothing had happened, that she hadn't changed, that she still is who she always had been.

Sylas said it didn't matter where she was or if she falls to pieces, that she's the same person deep down. But that's not true, either.

She *was* someone different, and she hadn't learned who that was. She wasn't sure she liked who she was now.

She floated between the mansion, the sculpture that was an impostor, Phoebe who was somehow so steady in who she was in the midst of evil, and the circus—Nick, Analiese, Sullivan even. She put on masks with each one, or at least she tried to. With Phoebe she was the steady constant. With Nick she was whimsical and carefree. With the Trenchers she was stoic and poised. But with each, the mask fell short—it didn't fit properly. The more she tried, the more she failed.

Analiese was more reasonable. Analiese said she could be wherever she wanted and whoever she wanted. Analiese said that who we were affects who we are, but that doesn't mean that's *all* we are, either.

And that's a bit closer to how Julia felt.

She looked down and held out her arms. She took a finger and traced over the scars that encircled her, evidence of what her past had left behind.

There was a piece of her she *hadn't* left behind, she couldn't leave behind. But there was a piece of her that *had* left, too; she couldn't find it again, and she wasn't sure if she wanted to or not.

It would take time. And the battered sculpture who looked out at the world resembled a state of naïveté. She was too jaded now for the outlook she'd once had.

# 16

AECHAELINE SCOWLED as she peered out the window. Through the yard and across the road sat a police car. Watching.

A stakeout on their place. That couldn't be good. "She's back…"

"Hmph…?" Max asked.

RaeChaeline rolled her eyes, walked over and pulled the tape off Max's mouth. "That cop," she clarified. "Didn't take the bait."

"Fancy's idea clearly didn't work," he said.

"Fancy's idea?! *Fancy's?* You're the one that forced and twisted things against Fancy's directives."

Max offered a sheepish smile. "What are we supposed to do now?"

"You're supposed to sit tight and leave it to me for once," RaeChaeline said. "I need to think without your hare-brained ideas getting in the way. Again."

"Just trust me!" Max insisted.

RaeChaeline's brows furrowed. "Then earn it!"

Max slouched, reluctant yet resigned. "At least…switch to ribbon or something so it doesn't hurt so much."

"As you wish, your highness," RaeChaeline muttered. "Whatever's most comfortable, that's what really matters here." She picked up the duct tape, then folded part of it over, sticking it to itself. Then, she yanked the tape off Max's arms (he responded with a yelp or two), wrapped the new material around Max's wrists, held the ends tightly together, and wrapped the remaining sticky tape around the end. It was a bit clumsy, but at least it wouldn't rip his hair out and maybe he'd whine a bit less. His mouth, though—she couldn't risk that. She taped it shut again.

She turned and peered out the bay window, deep in thought.

"We have time," she reassured. "She isn't approaching, which means she doesn't have what she wants. Yet. We still could burn this place down and claim it was an accident."

Max's eyes widened.

"Hmm, you're right," she said, though Max hadn't said anything and she hadn't even glanced his way. "What a waste of a cushy home for us. There's gotta be another way."

She walked over to the door, opened it, then turned back. Checked her reflection.

"I'm not gonna react, Max. That's not how to use this. We have to be proactive. We have to think ten steps ahead, even if the next step isn't one we'd like." Then, she exited and shut the door.

*Obsession and desperation can have a tenuous relationship. You're never sure if it's one or the other, and sometimes it doesn't matter. It's all-consuming.*

*So when the trials didn't work, Gep wouldn't accept it. Of course he wouldn't. So he pulled in his frenemy Viel, showed him the discovery against RaeChaeline's better judgment.*

*Viel wanted to try again. And so did Gep.*

*But this is where things go awry. Where obsession and desperation claw into business they never should be in, and decide that perhaps the experiment would only work on humans. Perhaps the only way to progress is to risk it all.*

*So Gep went under. He wasn't about to let Viel go first, and Viel was more obsessive or desperate to one-up Gep than to make a scientific breakthrough, anyway.*

*"Don't do this, RaeCh whispered.*

*"Don't fail me," Gep whispered back.*

*He went under, and RaeCh helped Dr. Viel operate.*

*When Gep came out of it, when he recovered, nothing seemed different.*

*They didn't realize it at first. It was too subtle for that.*
*In fact, they'd thought they failed.*
*"Sometimes science doesn't give what we'd expect."*
*They were right. Sometimes instead it takes.*

# 17

ENKINS WATCHED THE WOMAN nonchalantly peek from behind the curtain. Couldn't she have peeked out furtively, eyes dancing back and forth in fear? No, not this woman. It took more than threats to ruffle her.

Then, they met eyes. At least, Jenkins thought they might have. It was too far away to say for sure, and the woman didn't react. Then the curtains closed. She sighed. Nothing to see here now.

Jenkins almost left. There was nothing to do here but wait. She didn't like waiting, but she couldn't bear to leave empty-handed. Thankfully, she wouldn't have to.

A few moments later, the woman opened the door. She came out, down the walkway, and crossed the road, straight for Jenkins' car.

She was headed her way. She was headed *here*. Jenkins wondered if she should be worried, afraid. But she'd pretend not to be rattled. She'd trained for such moments. Jenkins opened the car door.

"Just what do you expect to get out of this?" the woman said. "A waste of county resources and tax dollars on the word of what...? A couple glamorized news articles to sell more papers."

Jenkins shook her head. "News articles *write* the stories, they don't make the stories."

"Any journalist worth their salt would disagree."

"What do you want?" Jenkins asked.

"I want to be left alone in my own home." The woman was clipped, pointed. Suspect? Couldn't be sure.

Jenkins decided to put her on the defensive. "That's funny; I heard this isn't yours."

The woman shrugged. "It is for now."

She wasn't taking the bait. Or had nothing worthwhile to offer.

Jenkins pursed her lips, sighed, then turned her key in the ignition. "Look, those notes may have critical information on a cold case. I'm not just gonna turn a blind eye. But if I get those notes and they don't point straight back to you, I got no need to be here. Know what I'm saying?"

The lady looked up and took a deep breath.

"Have a good day." And Jenkins closed the door, put the car in drive, and drove away. She looked in the rearview mirror. The lady still stood there, watching.

# 18

OBODY HAS SEEN YOUR NOTES. YES?"

Max grunted under the tape.

"Just nod or shake your head."

Max rolled his eyes and muttered something she couldn't make out.

RaeChaeline gave an exasperated groan. "Yes. Or. No."

Max still said nothing.

RaeChaeline ripped the tape off. "If you say one word Fancy doesn't like..."

"My notes from after... after everything... No one saw those. My notes from before I don't know."

She put the tape back over his mouth. "Obviously. We're going to assume Jenkins doesn't know anything about your before."

"Mph Mm?" She lifted the tape, and Max repeated himself. "Are we?"

"We are." RaeChaeline put the tape back over his mouth, then left the room.

Max waited. I mean, what else could he do when he's tied up?

Twenty minutes later she returned, paper in hand. She grabbed his chair and dragged it with great effort to the dining room table. She set blank sheets of paper in front of him, and a pen next to that. Then, she set piles of notes on the other side. His notes. The notes no one had seen. Or so he'd thought.

"Mmph!" he exclaimed through the tape.

"Found them," she said. "But lucky for you, I'm not totally cruel. I'm not going to ask you to burn them again. We're just going to create new copies that tell the story the way we want the cops to go. Away from us."

She pulled out a knife and cut the ties to his wrists, then handed him the pen and leaned toward his ear. "Clock's ticking. Let's write this story *our* way this time."

# 19

HOEBE RUBBED THE KEY between her fingers with curiosity. When had that gotten there? She wondered if it belonged to the door in the ceiling she couldn't get off her mind.

Sometimes it worked like that. She wouldn't remember details, but her body instinctively knew what to pay attention to, what mattered, what choice to take based on the past. She kept the fragmentation of her memories a secret in general, yes; but even with those who knew her lost memories, she hid that there were other things she knew without knowing. Better to think she knew everything or nothing than to twist what little she did know to their own advantages.

So when Dr. Evil had wrapped up for the night, she cracked a window by the entry. She exited the building and bade farewell, then watched from a shrub by the entryway 'til he disappeared into his gargantuan building that passed for a home. She continued to rub the key, to keep the memory fresh of why she was waiting. She whispered "a door in the ceiling" over and over to keep her focus right.

And then, she snuck back in. She crawled through the window conveniently left ajar next to the entryway and approached the dark hall. She couldn't turn on the lights for fear of being seen. She couldn't see the door in the ceiling, couldn't even remember it. But she felt it. She knew it was there.

Phoebe searched the closet and found a ladder. It took a few tries to set it up in just the right spot, climb the steps, and feel the crack in the ceiling. She traced the outline with her fingers until she felt a bolt, and then the lock that begged for a key. She shivered with wonder. Whatever was up here, it'd been calling to her. A memory she'd lost or a memory she needed, it was on the other side of this door. And she had to know what it was.

She reached the key above her head and unlatched the lock, then creaked the door open a crack.

Suddenly her fingers bristled as something scurried across it, and she shook her hand. The key fell to the ground with a clatter, and she brushed her hand on her skirt while balancing precariously on the ladder.

A spider.

It fell to join the key, she supposed. Probably wasn't the only one up in this decrepit attic, though, and she braced herself for more creepy crawlies.

Once the door was open, she felt through the fine, sticky cobwebs and found rungs she could climb, assuming they wouldn't break with the weight after so long in neglect. She pulled herself up with grunt after grunt, but she made it and collapsed on the floor of the room she'd been needing to get to for so long.

She was ready to find out why.

"Oh. You're not...him. Hello." A voice said in the darkness.

Phoebe felt critter legs scurry across her own, and she brushed them away while pushing herself to her feet. "Who are you?"

There was a clicking sound, and then a lightbulb bathed the room in a dim yellow glow. Phoebe looked at her surroundings: piles and piles of boxes, some open and spilling their contents.

In the middle of the room, holding the string that must have turned on the light, was a girl a bit younger than her. The girl had curly, wild hair that hadn't been tamed in a long time, and crawling in and out of her hair were bugs—no, not bugs. Spiders. The spiders would hide in her hair and scurry out across her arms, her legs, her torso, her face.

More than that, spiders covered the room, some scurrying, some crawling, some leaping over each other. It had to be hundreds, perhaps even thousands. Spiders of every size imaginable, from a glimmer of dust to the size of her head.

Phoebe didn't necessarily mind the stray spider here or there, but she'd discovered there was a line.

"Who are you?" Phoebe asked again.

"Intruders answer first." A large spider crawled from between her hair and neck, onto her cheek. "Wouldn't want to miss an introduction and upset my little pets."

# 20

RAECHAELINE DOESN'T WRITE. She sits there, thinking. Then she paces, thinking. She grabs food and brings it back. Thinking. She falls asleep and wakes up. Thinking.

I am impatient, not just because that's in my nature (I'm pretty sure Jasper would concur on that one), but also because I am still tied up. RaeChaeline is a more slow, methodical type.

I write on a piece of paper: *I have an idea.*

"Oh no no, I've heard your ideas before," RaeChae says.

I write again: *Fancy! It's a good one.*

RaeChaeline rubs the bridge of her nose. "Fine. This I gotta hear."

I scribble as quick as I can before she changes her mind.

RaeChaeline looks over my shoulder and reads along: *We need to send the cops back to the apartment. Tell them again that the dead guy is there alive, and this time the notes will act as a sort of proof.*

RaeChaeline laughs. "You think they'll just believe that because it's in your notes? And that you hid that this whole time? I thought you didn't wanna end up in prison."

I fold my arms together on the table and slump my face into them.

RaeChaeline pats my shoulder. "Don't you worry. Fancy will work this all out in no time. You just sit there, and when she's ready you'll put your handwriting to good use." Then, she sits there some more. Still thinking.

Until one day...

So, I begin to write. Not this. I write something old, and yet somehow new. It had RaeChaeline twists to it. Her own spin on the story. Not the story you read. A new and improved one that would lead to a fall guy that presumably isn't me.

It went something like this.

I was hired by RaeChaeline to investigate the whereabouts of her former crew. She believed they were in danger after that night, that the fire was an attack.

And, I poorly investigated. She wasn't about to make me some genius detective, said it had to be believable. One of these days she's gonna have to stop insulting me.

So I investigated around. Mr. and Mrs. Trencher had predictably escaped with their child, Julia. None of them knew what happened to the others. I found Ferg's apartment, with him alive, go figure. He pointed me in the direction of Dinah's Diner, where Phoebe was. Nick had joined her by that time, escaping in some freak power malfunction at Psych Institute. And lastly, Analiese. She had been holed up here, in this mansion, laying low. All of them spooked because Geppetto was missing after a threat from an old pal—Dr. Viel. We know of him as Dr. Evil, but apparently he has another name that cops would be more likely to find him by. The things RaeChaeline knows!

It all ends with having to plant some notes that incriminate this man and don't incriminate her. She has me write that she'd hired me to investigate while she went undercover in his lair—I mean clinic—and been unable to find anything. (Hey, she made herself seem a little dull herself in the story so she'd be less suspect! Can I say she's doing the same for me? Please?)

I sneak into the lair—clinic—and instead of being captured and tortured by RaeChaeline—which as you may have read is what actually occurred in my notes—instead I find suspect books about the brain and psychology and such. I mean, I really did, but that's what she has me focus on. Dr. Evil's notes. I mean, Dr. Viel's notes. (She has me write the notes multiple times because I keep messing up these details because no one can just give me the actual facts to write these lies from. [Insert exasperated sigh here.])

She also has me note the creepy freezer and claim it is locked up solid. It wasn't locked in real life, just the front door. And the back door, but that hardly counts when it wouldn't latch right. Anyhow, she makes it seem a little more secure than it already is.

Then we just need filler content, a bunch of "fluff" notes. She seems to think that putting that note in the midst of a whole bunch of nothing will get the cops onto this Evil guy, which apparently these circus people despise even though they flit about him like he's their sustenance. I mean, he is their sustenance. Their circus is on his land and he's sponsored it for whatever laughable reason.

I wonder if him and Gep are like Ferg and me—two people who are volatile and utterly dependent, who can't escape each other as much we try. Until now. I've found my path, and it seems like RaeChaeline is ready for Gep to have his. Dismissing the whole he's dead thing of course. She's still in denial about that.

And so, we've circled around to who she wants to be the fall guy. She doesn't just need Dr. Evil to be the murderer. The story still needs a corpse, a victim, too.

The problem is, everyone that died is now alive and the cops don't know it. Except for Gep, which is the one dead guy that RaeCh wants to be alive. See where I'm going with this? The fall guy has no victim that RaeChaeline would be okay with, and she needs one. She needs one dead guy to come to life and one live guy to die in an incriminating way.

And what RaeChaeline wants, as far as I can tell, she always gets. Not to mention her extra super word power on her side.

Someone was gonna die. And I need to stay on her good side to make sure it's not me.

# 21

HE CLOCK IS TICKING. The cops could show up with a search warrant at any time, and the notes are only one part of the plan.

There's still incriminating evidence to be sure is in Dr. Evil's lair without getting caught there ourselves. And there's some alleged witnesses to be sure our stories all line up perfectly. Most importantly, there's still Gep to raise and a guy to kill (the identity of which is to be determined, I think, unless she just isn't telling me as the sacrificial Isaac, which is quite possible).

RaeChaeline is on the move. She was done preparing and ready to take action. She drags out all her preparations and planning, but once she's ready, she strikes fast. Which is good, because did I mention the cops could show up for the notes at any moment?

I don't do good on a deadline, especially when the deadline is an unknown imminence, and especially when I'm with someone so particular about the details. She doesn't do "winging it," and that's all I know how to do.

She instructs me on exactly what I can and cannot write. She writes something of her own on notecards, places them precisely in envelopes, puts names on the front. I try to read, but she won't let me. I count one, two, three, four.

She checks that my legs are still tightly bound to the chair, then grabs the envelopes and leaves the room, heading toward the door. I call out to ask where she's going, but she only responds with a warning to keep the notes on track. Then the door shuts with a heavy, ominous thud.

I think about escaping, of course I do. But, she probably knows I would, knows I could, and she lets me stay anyhow. Really I'm not bound by the chair; I'm bound by the impending search warrant. And as little as I trust RaeChaeline even now, she's still my best shot of getting out of this. So I stay put and write exactly how she'd directed.

A few hours later she returns, and I'm clenching and releasing my fist. "Finished so soon?" she asks.

"I got a few days done." I rub my wrist to no avail.

"A few days?! A few days..." RaeChaeline sighs and plops into a seat. "We don't have time for you to do hand yoga or whatever that is."

"It's cramping; I'm just taking a break."

"You can take a break when you're sitting in a prison cell for the murder of your roommate who's alive and well. If your hand cramps will cause you to go to prison, push through and you can cut off your hand when it's all said and done, for all I care."

I scowl. "It can't look like I was writing under duress as the penmanship gets worse over time. I'll get it written, just ease up."

She smirks. "Look at you, thinking for once. I'm so proud." She picks up the notes I'd already written and "hmm"s her approval on a couple and squinches her nose up on more, tossing them in a crumple on the floor. I slump my head onto the tabletop with a sigh.

"You'll get it," she reassures. "But go shower; we got an appointment we don't wanna be late for."

I lift my head and look at her quizzically, but she just smiles. I shrug, stand, and go to take a step before the chair reminds me. I trip to the floor, the chair clattering with me. I'm still tied up. Right.

RaeChaeline laughs, takes out a knife from somewhere and cuts me loose.

# 22

PHOEBE DIDN'T HAVE A TOTALLY BLANK MEMORY. She saw things, things some would claim she was never supposed to see. So while Clementine and her pals demanded an introduction, Phoebe didn't need one. Phoebe saw the army of spiders and the girl with the wild hair—Clementine. She saw a moment of their future or past, and with that she knew one more thing about Clementine than Clementine knew about her.

Leverage, you could say.

"Clementine," Phoebe said. "I mean no harm. I..." She almost said she had no idea that Clementine was up here, but she wasn't entirely sure that was the truth. "I don't believe we've met."

"No, of course," Clementine said. "Anyone would remember meeting Clementine and Claude."

"Claude?"

Clementine bobbed her head and gestured about. "Claude."

Phoebe looked around the attic, but saw no one. She swiped at the spider crawling up her neck, then realized...Claude.

"Do you mind, ehmm... Which one is Claude?" Phoebe asked.

Clementine laughed. "Which one... Which one, indeed. Don't suppose you have a name?"

Phoebe shuddered. "Phoebe."

"Ahh yes. I've heard of you."

"Oh?" Phoebe wondered. "Heard what?"

"You're helping Dr. Viel get back his nemesis."

"And what are you doing?"

"Doing? What, up here?" Clementine laughed again. "Just enjoying the ambience you could say. The penthouse suite, right Claude?" A spider the size of Phoebe's fist crawled across Clementine's cheek, and she stroked it lightly with her finger. "Aww, darling."

Phoebe didn't know what to expect when she climbed into the attic. She certainly didn't expect a girl or spiders for pets. And she didn't know what to make of this girl who seemed just fine and dandy being up here. "You were locked up here, though. The door was locked."

"No one simply locks Claude away, dear." The spider poked its leg into her mouth, and she picked him up and sat him in her wild hair, nudging a couple smaller ones out of his way, then holding out her hand to show just a pinprick of one creeping along her pointer. "Have you seen the size of some of these? They can fit through anything."

"Not Claude," Phoebe said. "You. How long since you've been out?"

"Out where? Of this room?" She traipsed past Phoebe to the ladder. "I've been waiting for you, of course."

Clementine took a few steps down. Swarms of spiders led the way, trailed behind, and everywhere in between.

"Coming, Phoebe?"

"But how did you…"

"You of all people should know there's ways of knowing things you shouldn't. Right?"

Phoebe went to grab a railing, but the spiders were in the way.

"Don't crush Claude if you want to stay on our good side, now."

So Phoebe waited. She waited quite awhile as Clementine smirked at her from below. As the ladder was clearing up, Clementine added in, "Come on now, do hurry. You received a titillating invite while you've been snooping about."

Sure enough, Clementine was waving an envelope in her face once she'd descended. It said *Phoebe* on it in handwriting she wasn't sure if she should recognize.

"Where'd you get that?"

"From Claude."

"Claude can write?"

Clementine smirked. "Don't be silly. What is this, Charlotte's Web?"

Phoebe opened it. The big top. Tonight. But no explanation as to why or from whom. Phoebe's stomach tightened. She shuddered. Her body remembered something, but her memory didn't know what.

"Let's go. We'll be just shy of fashionably late; it's perfect."

Clementine led Phoebe, and Claude led Clementine. Past the mansion and into fields, toward the circus. It was too late for the show, too late for spectators. Just late enough for a clandestine rendezvous.

"Watch your step." Clementine nudged a spot with her toe. "That's where the body was found."

Phoebe avoided the spot, and was awed to see the spiders giving it a wide berth as well.

Clementine pointed further back into the circus lot. "Over there is where the fire started. But *we* are going to the big top. It's bigger than the last one, if you remember. From your visions."

Phoebe didn't respond. Clementine already knew more than she should.

They walked past the circus wagons, including Phoebe's where she still stayed. The spiders arrived at the big top first, and climbed the outside, slowly transforming it from the muted colors in the shadows into deep black. Clementine plucked at the tent opening and allowed Phoebe to enter first, then followed.

Analiese, Sullivan, and Nick were there.

"Who called this meeting, Phoebe? This isn't funny."

Phoebe held her hands up in a shrug.

"Who's this?"

"Clementine," she said. The spiders crawled up the inside of the tent and poured in from the top as well, until it was one black swarming mass. "This is Claude," Clementine added with a gesture at the brood.

"And what's this all about, Clementine? Why bring us all here?"

"Oh, I didn't. But the host will be arriving shortly."

Just then, RaeChaeline and Max entered the tent. RaeChae scrunched up her nose at the spiders and rolled her eyes in disgust. "Who brought company?"

The tent opened for one last person: Julia.

"Anyone else, your highness?" Analiese crossed her arms and glared at RaeChaeline.

"We're all here," RaeChaeline said. "...and then some. This was an invitation-only shindig."

"Yeah, yeah, we won't tell anyone about your murder plan, just get on with it," Clementine said.

"Murder?!" Max said.

"Haven't we seen enough murder for one circus?" Nick looked to Analiese for support, and she nodded.

"I can neither confirm nor deny that in this...mixed company." RaeChaeline looked at Clementine, then around the group at each one in turn. "What I can confirm is that the police are chomping for someone to go down for it all, and it's about time we give them that someone."

"Who?" Julia said. "No one knows..."

"Max knows, but that's besides the point. Right, Max?"

Max gulped and gave a forced smile. "Right?" he squeaked.

"I'm merely suggesting we each do our little part to give the cops the evidence and witness statements they need to bring justice that is long overdue."

"You're gonna have to do more than suggest and spit it out, RaeChae." Analiese stepped forward. "Who exactly are you taking out?"

"Dr. Evil."

"How convenient." Analiese came up to RaeChaeline's face and looked her eye to eye. "Still doing Gep's dirty work when he's not even here."

RaeChaeline gritted her teeth. "He'll be here to see it. I guarantee."

"'Sides danger and prison, what's in it for us?" Nick said. "Why should we care?"

"Agreed," Analiese said. "We just got this circus back up, a tour starting in a couple weeks. We'll be outta here before they pin anything down, and the trail will go cold all over again. Just like last time."

RaeChaeline stepped around Analiese to see the group again, and began pointing at each, starting with Max: "You don't think they'll find a way to lock you up if they keep digging?"

Max's gaze fell to the ground.

Then RaeChae turned to Phoebe. "Find out more about what happened here?"

To Analiese: "What *happens* here?"

Next Nick: "What we do?"

RaeChae turned uncomfortably to Clementine and Sullivan. "Who we are?"

Finally she studied Julia. "Or what we've lost?"

RaeChae gave a painful, practiced smile. "There's always another prison cell or another test lab for the likes of us if they dig too deep. We all know it."

"What do we need?" Julia said. "If...If we choose to go along with this."

"Just a fall guy and a story."

"Dr. Evil is the fall guy," Analiese said. "Right?"

"No, we already have him. We need a corpse."

Phoebe furrowed her brow. "You mean Gep...?"

Analiese chimed in. "We have one missing corpse that the cops are aware of. We have one corpse that the cops are not aware of. It's a simple trade really, only we all know that RaeChae wouldn't let us get off that easy." Analiese looked at RaeChaeline. "Would she?"

"Heavens, no. I told you. Gep will live to see this day."

"Live again, huh? You still believe it?"

"I have no choice..."

"So do tell me. Who dies so that Gep can live and win your little game?"

"The corpse that went missing. Obviously."

Max cleared his throat. "Uhmm excuse me. You mean, you plan on killing...? You plan on killing him? We just raised him from the dead."

RaeChae smiled at him patronizingly. "That was a mistake. I thought you wanted to know your past, but turns out you changed your mind."

"So maybe I change my mind again!" Max said.

RaeChaeline sighed. "The point is...don't worry about who the fall guy is. We just all need to get our story straight. We need Gep's body out of Dr. Evil's lair when the cops show up, another body in its place, and most importantly, Dr. Evil to go down for it. Who's in?"

Max cautiously raised his hand.

RaeChaeline raised an eyebrow at him.

Naively, he took that as permission to speak. "I'm a bit new here, so bear with me. But there isn't by chance a Dr. Also-Evil that could be the corpse, is there?"

"You mean an Assistant Evil perhaps?"

"Oh, that's too perfect," Max said. Then, "No. I wouldn't dare."

Analiese stepped forward, inches from RaeChae. For the first time ever, Max saw RaeCh flinch, but to her credit she didn't budge.

"You're not the queen bee around here anymore," Analiese said. "You don't get your way, not this time. Take your posse and schemes. We won't be your fall guys anymore."

"Analiese, this isn't a game..."

"It's never been a game, RaeChae. It's our lives. And I see yours clearly now."

RaeChaeline finally stepped back, brows furrowing. Was that confusion? Anger? Or...fear?

"All the years, all the life. You're positively frail. Your mask is coming off."

"I don't have the privilege of creating a new one whenever I want," RaeChaeline said, voice faltering. "Let's get outta here."

She turned and Max followed.

Clementine dramatically gave a slow clap.

"What are you and your critters still doing here?" Analiese said.

"Oh, marvelous performance," Clementine said. "Five stars. But I didn't hear any plan from this crew, so she'll be back, and for your sake hopefully before the cops. Keep that in mind." Then Clementine smiled at Phoebe. "Let's get back. We have a long day ahead of us tomorrow."

Phoebe waved at the others and followed Clementine.

Clementine pranced through the fields. "It's so lovely being in this wide open expanse. So exhilarating and refreshing." Then she slowed and frowned. "But exhausting. How do you all do this every day?"

"What, a clandestine rendezvous? This would be the first I remember."

"Not that," Clementine said. "Interact. With people."

"You interact with, uhmm, Claude, don't you?"

Clementine waved her hand in dismissal. "He doesn't count."

"Because he doesn't talk back?"

"Doesn't-" Clementine laughed. "Doesn't talk back? Claude talks more than I do, silly."

"Oh, of course."

Clementine smiled like she had just remembered an inside joke. "Claude gets me, and I get him. Everyone else I just pretend."

Phoebe nodded. "That makes sense, I think. I pretend sometimes, too."

Clementine squinted her eyes. "Sometimes, hmm? Seems to me you haven't stopped pretending since... Well, you won't remember."

"Maybe."

After minutes of silent walking, Phoebe and Clementine—and we can't forget Claude—arrived back at the lab.

Clementine held up a key. "You didn't remember the key, but Claude did. Set it on that end table to not arouse suspicion."

Phoebe accepted the key, but Clementine didn't wait for her to put it back in its place. Clementine walked past the front office and into the hall.

Phoebe dumped the key where she hoped it should be, then briskly followed. "What now?"

"Now, we sleep. Just don't lock the attic, and we'll see you in the morn'." Clementine winked, then her and Claude climbed the stairs and vanished into the shadows above.

# 23

ANALIESE STOPPED JULIA AT THE ENTRY. "Don't do this," she said. "I see you, wanting to help. Wanting to..." She clasped her fingers together and looked down. *Belong*, she wanted to say. But when she had that available to offer and held it out of reach even yet, she couldn't rub it in. Not now. Not with what's at stake.

"I get it," Julia said. "The contract is broken. 'That's the end of that.' I should stay out of it."

"You should." Analiese put her hand to her gut, where the guilt had set in like a stone. "But not because of that. I told Nick things are about to get worse. Remember? And it's still circling. RaeChae, Dr. Evil, the cops, murder..."

Julia clasped her hands and looked down at them. "I shouldn't get away scot-free."

"We can handle it," Analiese claimed, though she wasn't convinced. But, she didn't need to convince herself. She needed to convince Julia.

Julia shrugged. "I can help."

It wasn't gonna work. Playing nice usually didn't, Analiese had found. She gritted her teeth. "You can't help," she spat. "That's what got us into the mess. You'd do Nick and all of us more good if you stay away. Don't you get it!?"

Julia bit her lip. Nodded.

Why did she always have to play mean? Analiese sniffed. "Good."

RAECHAELINE THROWS A PAN onto the stovetop. She's steaming and wants something to take it out on, I guess.

I assumed our dear volatile Fancy 1.0 could get under Fancy 2.0's skin; they were never buddy buddy. But RaeChaeline could play it off usually. I guess it was that mask metaphor they were talking about. RaeCh would be the picture of calm and serenity in situations that had to make her bristle underneath. She kept it deep, deep, deep down somewhere inaccessible.

But not now. It's bubbling up. The oil and kernels make their pop sounds as an external presentation of her internal demeanor. Her jaw is set, trying to hold it in, but her face betrays it with twitching. Her arms tremble.

I've never seen her so unsettled. And that unsettles me. I don't have many eggs and I'm kinda putting them all in the RaeChaeline basket. I'm not even sure there's another basket to put them in. And I can't lose my eggs.

I cautiously grab a bowl before she could clang it onto the table. She glances up with maybe a hint of gratitude or contempt. Who can tell with her? She puts her hand on mine where it's holding the bowl. I sure hope it's gratitude. I've never noticed the wrinkles forming on her hands 'til that moment. She isn't as young as she let on; her years are getting to her. And maybe she's self-conscious of that with Analiese's jabs earlier. So I don't comment. I just step away.

She dumps the popcorn into the bowl, then shoves a handful into her mouth like that would push all the emotions down.

Usually opening my mouth doesn't help, but that's never stopped me. So... "Fancy, they'll come around."

"Who says we need them?" she says between chomps. "We've got Gep on our side, remember."

"We've got..." I frown. "Yeah. But more importantly, Fancy can get the whole lot of them to her side. Remember?"

"Why?"

"It's what we...It's what me and Fancy have been practicing for." I smile as an idea sparks. "Ya see, I'm a survivor. Barely, but that's beside the point. Fancy, though... Fancy is more than a survivor. She's a dreamer. And when she's got some hare-brained idea, she's also got plan B, C, D, and all the alphabet lining up at her disposal. What Fancy wants, Fancy gets."

RaeCh squints. "Carry on..."

"I'm not talking about no OG Fancy. I'm talking about this Fancy. The Fancy who's been planning ahead and setting herself up for success for months. It's not over. It's just starting. You taught me that." I point at her.

She waves her hand. "Okay, okay, stop with the second person nonsense before Fancy uses it against you. Eat some popcorn."

I smile and grab a bite. "What's next, Fancy.

*Then, there were too many coincidences. Too many things said that came true. Not everything; that'd be too obvious. But enough. Enough would come true to make RaeCh cock her head and Gep's eyes widen.*

*An arbitrary "You can't keep working so late," and surprisingly he listened and, if not in time for supper, at least got to bed at a decent hour.*

*A playful "You'll cause a scene if you keep making eyes at me in public" causing a fight to break out.*

*A force was working its way into the universe, and it all started with this one patient zero. As I said, it wasn't everything. They couldn't figure out what it was.*

*They would try words that seemed to so certainly make this magic transpire, and nothing would happen, or worse the words would be twisted into a shape they never intended. And they would say something so innocuous it should be meaningless, then notice its workings like a clock ticking, slowly but surely shaping Gep's life and those around him.*

*They kept it secret. It was too powerful, too dangerous.*

*But Viel wasn't entirely dense, and he began to notice, too. And as the pattern emerged, he smiled. He knew just what made Gep tick.*

# 25

NOTHER DAY CLOSER. Closer to cops banging down the door and taking my notes, fake or otherwise. Another day steadily counting down from an unknown number, counting down not to an explosion but to my possible imprisonment. (Is it any different?)

RaeCh had me up late past the little reunion, writing all the notes I messed up earlier. She finally let me sleep, but not long enough because there she is now pacing and muttering to herself.

I groan and sit up from the couch I'd collapsed on halfway to my room. "Good morning," comes out hoarsely.

"Afternoon," she corrects.

"Right. What'd I miss?"

"Fancy thinks she has the words."

I push myself to my feet and smile. "Oh? To make the next reunion more endearing?"

Fancy cocks her head. "More pliable, yes."

"Need I remind you these are humans, not pottery."

Fancy scoffs. "They serve a function, nothing more."

"You like them, and that scares y-" She covers my mouth, and I am again thankful this is a different Fancy who couldn't treat me literally like pottery. Though she has her own tricks.

"So I like them, but you will not finish that sentence," she says.

I nod.

"But more importantly, they'll like me." She scrunches her face. "Right?"

I step backwards for her palm to fall from my mouth, then clear my throat. "Say it more emphatically. And present tense."

She nods and furrows her brows in concentration. "They like me."

"Who?"

"Does it matter? Can't it be everyone?"

I shrug. "I don't know, Fancy doesn't seem the type to want stalker fans."

"Ahh, yes." She pauses. "Analiese. Julia. Nick. Phoebe. They…"

I wait.

But she doesn't continue. She slumps.

"They…?"

"They aren't Gep. I just want Gep."

"They're family too, right?" I say hopefully. "Family isn't perfect."

"Gep wasn't perfect. He just was mine. They belong to each other, but not to Fancy."

I pace for a moment, but the words come to me. "Fancy doesn't belong to them. That's different. Besides, every family is messy." I pause. "Gep really worth all this?"

RaeCh gets a far off look in her eyes remembering something and laughs. I realize it's that scoffing laugh she usually reserves for "inferior minds" like mine. She shakes her head. "He tried. Too scatterbrained. A true dreamer. I admire that in him. But he couldn't focus like me. His schemes fell short without me to tip the scales. He always had this sparkle in his eye when I found just the right domino to knock over. Ya know?" She frowned. "So no. He's not worth all this, objectively speaking. No one is. But that's not how humans work, that's not why we do things."

RaeCh sighs, purses her lips, then shakes her hands and head to attention like she's about to jump into a wrestling ring. "Okay, here goes... I got this. Analiese, Julia, Nick, and Phoebe's goals align with mine. They will see that."

I think a moment. "That should work...right?"

"Your guess is as good as Fancy's."

# 26

HEN PHOEBE RETURNED to the lab the next morning, she didn't remember what had transpired the night before. She didn't remember precocious Clementine or all-seeing Claude or a creepy attic or a secret meeting with the circus crew. Then again, she didn't really remember why she came to the lab in the first place, nor that it was a lab she was going to until she arrived. She didn't really remember the circus, not truly, only brief scenes to piece together a life that she couldn't be certain was future or past except by sheer instinct others may call a "guess."

When she arrived, she found a swarm of spiders throughout the office. She tiptoed around them as they meandered out of her path, more out of annoyance at the disturbance than welcoming politeness. She opened the door to the lab and found the spiders continued there, too. Clementine and Claude—that's when she realized their names—were at a standoff with Dr. Evil (whose name or nickname she did not recall, just his being).

"Lovely. You're here," Dr. Evil said with a sarcastic tone. "Care to share why you let out the riffraff?"

Clementine's fists clenched. "Don't you dare speak of Claude that way!"

"Oh, I assure you, I was not referring to the bugs."

Claude scurried forward and up Clementine's legs and arms, some perching in her hair.

"Don't listen to him," she soothed. "He doesn't know any better."

Phoebe stepped forward. "I can't say what I did or why."

"Of course, you wouldn't re-"

Clementine interrupted. "Claude and I are very capable of letting ourselves out. You underestimate us."

Dr. Evil glowered. "I perfectly estimate you and what you're capable of. Why do you think you were locked up?"

Clementine shrugged. "The attic was locked. We never were."

Dr. Evil trembled. "Delusion..."

"We're all here now," Phoebe said. "What of it?"

Dr. Evil pointed Phoebe's direction, more at the sound of her words than at her directly. "Now we're on the right track. What do you want?"

Clementine smiled. "We're going to crack this case wide open."

"Case? What case?"

"The mystery you all keep circling around and never face head-on," Clementine said. "Claude told me all about it."

"Of course he did," Dr. Evil sneered.

Clementine nodded and strokes a spider on her thumb. "The boy who wonders who he really is, for starters. Or the woman who wonders at her place in this world." She strokes the spider on her index finger next.

Dr. Evil shrugged. "Predictable."

Clementine squinted and touched Claude on her middle finger next. "There's another woman, who wonders who can see behind her facade."

"Don't we all?"

Clementine pulls her hand closer to her face and turns it to see the other side of her ring finger where Claude awaits. "Or there's the woman who wonders how to make the family she never got."

Dr. Evil remains unenthused by the theatrics. "Boring."

Finally Clementine arrives at her pinky finger. "How about the girl who wonders why she wants to be broken again, while the parents wonder how their brokenness has been put on display?"

Dr. Evil stifled a yawn as he nodded. "Better."

Clementine smiled and closer her hand into a fist as Claude's swarm enveloped her hand in brown fuzz. "But we mustn't neglect perhaps the most tired mystery of all: the doctor who wonders how to rid the world of mystery all together just to make a name for himself."

"That's more like it." Dr. Evil smiled. "*Now* we're getting somewhere."

Clementine tilted her head, opened her fist and waved it forward in a mock bow; it's as if she'd placed all her chess pieces exactly where she'd like them. "See Phebes. He just wants to suck all the fun out."

Phoebe, of course, did not see. She could see the match taking place in front of her, sure; but could not tell what game it was nor why this Clementine was winning. She only knew that she needed to be here longer for...something.

"Now that we've had our surprise entry," Clementine held up the key, yet again finding its way into her hands, "I hope you don't mind Claude and I holding on to this. Wouldn't want a problem with the locks, would we?"

Dr. Evil frowned.

A spider the size of a dinner plate gripped its legs like claws into Clementine as it climbed to her shoulder. She set the key in its outstretched front legs, then stroked a couple fingers between its eyes. "Come Phebes," she said. "We have a long day ahead of us."

"Doing what?" Phoebe asked.

"Solving mysteries."

Claude scurried out of the building, and Phoebe followed.

Just as Clementine was about to exit as well, she turned back to Dr. Evil. "Oh, and... don't even think of changing the locks. Claude would see, and you wouldn't want to upset him."

# 27

HERE ARE MERE DAYS IF NOT HOURS to turn over the notes and hope we have a case. You're thinking, that should be plenty, just write up some notes, in, like a couple hours here and there.

But writing comes slow, laborious, as much a labor of the mind as the poor hand that is cramped up now and can't go another day. Especially when there's a Fancy hovering over my shoulder telling me how incriminating my words sound and can't I just get it right for once. I'd thought I had too much self-doubt and self-deprecation as a writer already, but Fancy and the threat of jail take it to a whole new level.

Lying under oath. Obstruction of justice. Co-conspiring. Would it be called forgery to fake investigative papers if they're false, but still mine, but I'm not really an investigative journalist or private eye or whatever lie I last told? Not sure, but I would like the court system to not have to identify what sort of crime that is for me. We'll just leave it to my imagination.

Oh, yeah, and then there's the whole murder charge they or Fancy could end up dropping on me just for funsies.

In the meantime, I remind myself it's only days or hours imprisoned to Fancy's schemes, just for the hope of possibly staying out of a more permanent prison.

And just as I thought I'd get some peace and quiet to make more progress on the notes while Fancy sleeps in, a knock on the door interrupts. I groan. I've established I don't have time for this.

The knock recurs. Impatient.

It occurs to me that this could be the moment we've been dreading. The search warrant. I scramble to collect the papers into a semblance of something that could be turned over if needed. I hope they don't dig through the trash and find all the discarded pieces and catch us in our lie.

The knocking resounds. Again.

I walk down the hall. A bug scurries across the carpet and under a sofa. It should have been a warning to me, but I'm oblivious. I'm too busy seeing Jasper in the mirror. His eyes are wide, worried. He doesn't trust that I can handle this well, I suppose, so I try to nod assuredly at him.

Fancy catches me right at the door. "Who is it?"

"I don't know. I just got here."

"Well, be careful."

"I know, I know..."

She huffs and peeks in the mirror at herself, then nods satisfactorily. She doesn't notice Jasper there like I do.

I creak open the door. Phoebe and that new spidery chick are here. They smile. I smile back, but my eyebrows are raised.

Fancy grabs my shoulder and tries to peer out over me.

I open the door further for Fancy to see.

"Oh, it's you," she says, disappointed. Then walks away.

"Where you going?" I ask.

"To call pest control!"

"I'm sorry," I whisper to the ladies and spiders at our doorstep. "One moment."

I close the door to go talk some sense into Fancy, then I realize I have no idea what I'm going to say.

I crack open the door again. "Sorry, again... Why are you here?"

Clementine answers, "To discuss the terms of the proposal."

"Ahh." I nod, and close the door. "Fancy!"

I head back the direction I'd seen her go, to find her in the library with a book open on her lap at about the halfway point. She isn't reading—I've never seen her read anything but my notes. Such a drama queen.

"I thought we're trying to make friends," I begin.

"Not with bugs and wild eyes." She licks her finger then turns a page.

I step forward and touch the corner of the book. Fancy's eyes widen and she blinks up at me. Do I dare?

"Why not?" I ask. "The more allies the better."

She pulls the book back a few inches, just enough so I'm not touching it. "You said yourself I don't like stalker fans."

"She doesn't come across that way."

"The spiders sure stalk her."

I reach for the book again, but she slides back. "What about Phoebe?"

"She won't remember if we talked or not, anyhow." Fancy looks behind me and rolls her eyes. She tosses her book to the end table and pushes up and past me.

I catch her just as her foot hovers over a coin-sized spider in the entryway and pull her back.

"Don't touch me!" she says.

"Don't squish it! We don't need more enemies right now."

"I was just..." she pauses. "...testing it...or you. Or something. Doesn't matter." She sets her foot down on a piece of the floor thankfully not taken up by another creature.

I sigh. I almost rush back to grab the book before she could read it again, then remember: She wasn't actually reading it, and in the absence of this one there's plenty of other books she could choose to not read instead.

"Fine, go let them in!" she interrupts my thoughts.

Clementine enters the room, followed by Phoebe and the gang. "Thank you."

"How dare..." Fancy starts.

"You were just inviting us in, weren't you?"

Clementine giggles, but Fancy is unamused. "If you'd give me a chance to."

I butt in. "She means 'hi, welcome, make yourself at home.'"

Clementine smiles. "I'm Clementine." She waves around the space acknowledging the army she carries around. "This is Claude. You know Phoebe."

Phoebe smiles.

"We're here to join forces with your whole murder mystery plan thing."

Fancy plops down in the chair. "Thanks for the offer, but we don't need another headstrong female in this story."

Clementine's smile freezes.

Which makes Fancy perk up a bit, thinking maybe she has an edge. "Analiese and I have that covered."

Clementine blinks then jumps back in. "Oh, I'm not headstrong. Common mistake. Claude's the headstrong one here."

Phoebe interjects. "Hear us out, RaeChaeline. You of all people know how alliances can form from the most unlikely sources."

"I don't exactly recommend working with Dr. Evil just because I have to right now."

"I don't mean him." Phoebe looks over at me. My face grows hot as RaeChaeline makes the connection.

"Oh! Yes, I suppose working with him hasn't been a total disappointment."

I sigh. Almost a compliment.

Clementine perks up. "Yes, we can be an alliance like that. Only...not that. We'll avoid all the journaling and the memory loss, stick to the witty bickering. Deal?"

RaeChaeline sits straight in her chair, not quite ready to stand in welcome, but more interested, perhaps. She likes bickering. "I don't know you from an annoying mosquito buzzing about, or a flea. Say I say yes. Hypothetically. What would you be willing to do to prove whose side you're on?"

"It goes both ways. What would you do?"

"Absolutely nothing. I'm not for hire."

"What if we all just quit with the power play," I hazard. "We can work together. We need each other. Phebes and I are team players."

"You're my team player, and don't you forget it," RaeCh says.

"Of course."

"Boy has a point," Clementine says. "Tell ya what. I'll go recruit one of them others for you."

"I don't need you talking to them," RaeCh jumps in, quick to command the lead again. "I need you to get this boy's notes. Sentimental value and all."

"Notes?" Clementine waves her hand in dismissal. "Not a problem. From where?"

"Ferguson's apartment. You can use your sidekick as bait. Not the spiders, the other one. He's head over heels for her."

Phoebe's brows furrow. A memory she can't retrieve.

"Will be back in a jiffy." Clementine hooks her arm around Phoebe's then prances out of the room with Claude in tow.

"Why would you tell her that?" I ask. "Why would you trust her with the location of my notes?"

RaeCh kicks her feet up on the sofa and smiles. "Your notes aren't the test. Sure, it'd be a nice plus if you could stop worrying about the cops finding your old notes to build their case against you."

(Funny, I don't remember worrying about the cops finding my old notes. Now I do.)

"But that's the decoy to my true motives," RaeCh continues.

"Which are?"

RaeCh looks around the room, to the ceiling, to the floor. Just short of actually getting up off the sofa and looking underneath all the furniture. Presuming she isn't looking for humans hiding in the rafters, she must be worried about Claude. And perhaps for another human the search would be sufficient to put them at ease. But RaeCh trusts no one. "Not here. Isn't safe. She could have spies anywhere."

I pick up the paper and pen from the table and hold it out to her. "Do you need to write it down?"

She doesn't take it. "It's not safe."

"Spiders can't read!"

"We don't know if Claude is in actuality a spider."

"In case you haven't noticed, he's hundreds of them."

RaeCh huffs.

"So we're just not talking now? I gotta read your mind as to what the plan is?"

"Since when have I trusted you with the plan anyhow?"

I shrug. "You said it's not completely miserable that we're unlikely allies, so figure it's time to open up, RaeCh."

She freezes ever so momentarily. Her eyes widen as she looks at me, and I nearly see her lips quiver. But it's just a trick of the light, certainly.

"What'd I say?"

She pushes out of her seat and walks out of the room. "Fine," she hollers back at me. "Keep up. I'll take you somewhere safe to talk, but you won't like it."

I fold my arms. "Good."

But then, I remember. I'm almost giddy; I can't wait 'til later, so I rush ahead.

"First... Don't hate me," I start, because that's always a good way to convince someone not to hate you...

RaeCh is instantly suspicious. She squints.

"I got you something."

"A gift?" RaeCh laughs, but in a scoffing way, not a hooray-you-got-me-a-gift way. Oh, yeah. That's why I'm not quite all-the-way giddy. "When?"

"When you fell asle—doesn't matter. It'll help the grand plan."

RaeCh's soft squint transitions to a hard glare. "Who's the

brains of this operation? You're not supposed to think. Who am I kidding, you don't think, that's the problem. You just act, but—"

I hold out my gift.

She falls silent.

"Like it?"

Her face softens again. "You realize it's dead, right?"

I look at the small bird in my palm. "Oh, yeah. Obviously. It was dead when I found it."

"So you didn't just get me a pet for emotional support, right?"

"Really?" I sat the bird on the tabletop. "I'm not that dense. I found it in the yard and thought you could test on it."

"Test!?"

"Yeah, like words and stuff to figure out what to say for Gep. We're low on time now."

RaeCh balks at me. "You want me to bring this bird back to life?"

"Why not?"

"In the house?"

I roll my eyes. "Then take it outside!"

"I'm not touching that diseased thing."

I don't remind her that she's already touched an oozing human corpse with ease. Instead I pick the bird up off the table and take it out the back door. I set it in a flower pot. "Happy now?"

RaeCh hasn't followed me. I walk back in, and she's standing by the kitchen sink. "Go on. Wash up before you spread it around."

After, she has me scrub my hands and the table and nearly the entire house, 'til I promise I hadn't set it down anywhere else.

She sighs. "Fine. I'll try to bring the emotional support bird back to life, but I'm not nursing it back to health. If it dies again, that's on you."

"So what should we name it?" I ask. "Hope?"

She rolls her eyes. "Chance."

"You of all people know the importance of words."

RaeChaeline sighs. "I hate to say you're right..."

"Then don't." Gotta keep her on my good side as long as I can. "How about Phoenix?"

"We don't want the name to give a false advantage here. The name Gep doesn't mean 'rise again'."

"Hmm..."

"Discovery," RaeCh says. "We'll call it Discovery.

# 28

PHOEBE LOOKED ACROSS THE ROAD at the building. "So, what's the plan?"

Clementine plopped down under the tree that Claude had overtaken. "We wait." She leaned back against the tree and closed her eyes, Claude clearing a spot for her head by climbing onto her neck and shoulder. "Claude will let us know when it's safe."

Phoebe crouched, but didn't quite sit.

"Relax," Clementine said. "This'll be easy. Claude will let us know when it's empty, let us in, we'll grab the notes and be out in a jiffy."

"We're breaking in?"

"We're not breaking anything. Claude is letting us in. And it's not a crime for spiders to enter a home."

(Some readers would add "unfortunately" to the end of that sentence, but of course Clementine wouldn't and Phoebe is too polite.)

Phoebe pulled her hair back in a pile atop her head. "If we're gonna be here awhile... Why don't you tell me what you and Claude's grand plan is."

"Plan?"

"Sure. Everyone has a motive. What's yours?"

Clementine shrugged and shooed a fly away. "We're more 'in the moment' sorta folks. You understand."

Phoebe nodded. "Sure, I do. But you don't. You're angling for something."

"Oh? And just what do you see of me and Claude that tells you that?"

Phoebe pursed her lips and shook her head. "You first."

Clementine pushed herself up so fast you'd think Claude would be in trouble, but he shared her eagerness and scurried closer to Phoebe in sync with Clementine's movements. "Ooh, a secret for a secret? I'm intrigued."

Phoebe smiled.

Clementine raises an eyebrow. "What's in it for you if you won't even remember what we tell you?"

"That's not the secret I agreed to exchange."

Clementine considered her options a bit, furrowing her nose. It didn't take long to decide. "Okay, I'm in."

Phoebe gestured to Clementine. "Then, as I said, you first."

A spider the size of Phoebe's fist stretched out a leg toward her. Phoebe reached her hand down, and it crawled into her palm. "Claude doesn't bite, does he?"

"Only those he doesn't like. And only some with venom." Clementine waved her hand dismissively, and Claude settled in the grass for a story. "It goes way, way back..."

# 29

DON'T LIKE IT. RaeCh was right.

We are just a few turns away from the "somewhere safe to talk" when I realize. I covertly unlock my seatbelt while distracting with small talk. I reach for the door handle. Just as I pull the latch, she grabs my arm and pulls me back, and the door shuts before it hardly even opened.

"You asked to talk about it," she insists.

"There?! Really?"

"It's safe. You have to admit nothing can sneak in unbeknownst to us."

"I'm more concerned about sneaking out." I shudder, remembering how that happened last time. Technically, I still don't really know how. I know it took Nick, but he's not here, and if he was I probably wouldn't take that ride again anyhow.

"Look. My plan isn't the old Fancy's plan," she clarifies. "We can both get in and get out without any sneaking. Just smarts—"

I open my mouth to protest.

"—and thankfully I have enough smarts for the both of us."

I close my mouth. Think. Then say, "So, what's the plan?"

She parks the car. "Politely asking."

I nod. Open my door to climb out. She's climbing out, too. I glance at her, at the entry, at the car. Then I take off running, away from the building.

RaeCh laughs, then yells after me. "Max, I have something they want more than either or both of us."

I hesitate. Slow. Stop. "What do you have?"

"Gep."

I nod. That could maybe work. But I'm not just gonna traipse in hoping. She wouldn't give Gep up so easily. I turn and look at her; she's smirking. "I'm not just gonna go in there and put my life in Gep's hands. I've seen how that pans out, no offense."

"I'll go make the deal. You wait here. They don't even have to know you're here. Once I have the space secured, I'll bring you in."

"And a key," I counter. "We have a key. That's the only way."

"Of course." She nods, turns, and walks confidently in to the building like she owns the place. Really, she walks the world like she owns everything, so how could I doubt her? Oh, right. Because she treats humans like things she owns, too.

I open the car door and sit, waiting, hoping. Still not sure I'll actually walk into the building when it's time, but trying to work up whatever courage I have, just in case.

I can't say if it's minutes or hours later. Every moment was too quick and too long as I wrestle with myself. All I can say is after a time, Fancy opens a side door to the building and beckons me. I glance around, as if I could spot any danger from out here. The danger obviously is inside, where I'm supposed to be heading. I arrive at the door much too quickly.

Fancy seems to think otherwise. "What took you so long?! Get in here."

I bow my head in shame or fear or something, and I duck in. (No, the door is not so low that I needed to. It just happened.)

She pulls me down a hall, but I refuse to look up. I remember the lights flickering, I remember my body unformed and terror as I enveloped the building. Or almost the building. I didn't get that far I suppose, not that it mattered. I still was some eerie otherness I wouldn't want to remember. I was one with Nick and with darkness, here, and neither of us liked it.

RaeCh pulls me into a room and the door closes. I glance up and recognize the white walls and ceilings, though thankfully not as blindingly bright as before. Still, it's a prison. Then I remember... "You promised a key."

She waves it in her hand. "We're fine. More importantly, not a spider in sight. The seal on these rooms is impeccable to keep all manner of oddities from getting in or out." She tilts her head to the side. "'Cept Nick, I suppose. Should we be worried about the ventilation system?"

I roll my eyes. "You did not drag me all this way to worry about spiders in the vents..."

She pursed her lips but nodded. "I suppose the spiders can't crawl quickly enough to get here yet. I'll chance it."

"So what's your grand plan? What's this test for the newbie?"

"Phoebe, obviously. I told Clementine the way in was through Phoebe's broken little heart, and she eats that up and uses her to get into our good graces, well..." RaeCh lets out a throaty laugh. "We'll know just how far to trust her."

I scrunch my nose. "Phoebe. She's supposed to pick up that it's a bad thing my old roomie is into her?"

"He's not around. Of course she'll know. If he was worthy of Phoebe, he'd not be pining away for her *away from* her."

"Oh, obviously."

"It's a matter of the heart. You wouldn't understand."

"Goes to show how far you can trust me," I mutter.

"More importantly," RaeCh continues her scheming, waving the key in my face which was probably keeping me about as calm as I possibly could be in here. "She's the ticket. She thinks she's on our side, thinks she's helping us, and then wham!" She claps her hands together, and the key clatters to the floor.

I scoop it up. "She can't be the dead body. She doesn't match the corpse in the slightest, not to mention she's a she."

RaeCh nods. "That's why she's the perfect victim. She thinks she couldn't possibly be in jeopardy. She helps set up all the incriminating evidence at the lab since she lives there. And then, when the cops show up to search, they don't find Gep's corpse. They find Dr. Evil's. And who better to be the fall guy except the girl he had locked up in his attic with a bunch of creepy crawlies."

"Locked up?"

"Oh, yeah, you hadn't heard. She's some chick he's terrified of, had her up there forever. I told him it was overkill."

"Of course you knew about her."

"What? Claude would probably vouch for me or I wouldn't even let her on the team."

"You mean, let her on the team just to betray her."

"Exactly."

"Wouldn't Claude not allow her to be locked up?"

"Even better. If Claude really could help her out, just means one less thing for me to feel guilty about. Just temporarily locking up someone to get the heat off our trail, as agreed, so me and Gep can ride off into the sunset and you can... well, whatever you finally decide to do with your life." She shrugs.

"Assistant Evil showing her title off splendidly."

"Yeah, yeah. Just be glad I'm letting you out of here. Let's go."

I smile. "I'm the one with the key. Who says I'm letting you out?"

"You know that's not remotely in the realm of possibility."

I did. We both leave together, my stomach doing flip flops, and I'm not sure if it's from relief I'm actually leaving this place or if it's from guilt gnawing at me. I'm hoping the former; after all, I've already chosen my side.

# 30

T'S TIME," CLEMENTINE SAID.

Phoebe hadn't noticed any signal from Claude, but apparently there had been one.

Phoebe didn't remember what Clementine had told her. Nor did she remember if she'd told Clementine what she sees. She didn't even remember that they'd had a discussion to agree to the exchange.

But that's not why Phoebe asked. Not for the memories to be captured in her brain, but for the memories to be captured in her body, her senses, her spirit. Intuition, you might say. Gut instinct based on what she knew but didn't remember she knew.

So while her brain threw the memory out the window, it saved the impulses, the feelings, the impressions for later, with Clementine and Claude none the wiser. The one secret Phoebe shared with no one.

So, Phoebe, unaware of what had shifted within her, went along with Clementine and Claude toward the apartment.

"Claude is letting us in to get something important that belongs to someone else," Clementine whispered at the doorway. "But there's someone in there sleeping so we need to remain quiet."

Phoebe nodded.

Claude covered the door, including the knob, and seeped in through the edges and cracks that humans wouldn't even notice. On the other side of the door, the side no human was witnessing, Claude turned the latch. Claude cleared off of the doorknob, and Clementine turned the handle and opened the door. They were in.

"Thank you, Claude."

They tiptoed into the building. (You may be wondering if Claude tiptoed, which, kinda. Spiders do not have toes, but he was on the bristly tips for solidarity.)

Claude led them down the hall to a bedroom with a simple bed and dresser. Sheets of paper were strewn in a half moon facing the head of the bed. Claude took over the foot of the bed, and Clementine sat at the head. She lightly touched a page that had seen better days. The pages were crumpled, words streaked.

Phoebe touched her shoulder. "These yours?"

Clementine shook her head. "Claude keeps my secrets better than paper."

"Should we be reading this?"

Clementine looked up and smiled. "No." She gathered the paper into a pile.

She stood, and Phoebe turned toward the door, but a man stood in the doorway. "Phebes..."

Clementine sucked in her breath.

"I've been looking for you," the man said. "Wondering if you were...okay."

Phoebe smiled, but for the first time in a long time it wasn't a relaxed smile. It was tight, and refused to meet her eyes. "I'm...okay."

Clementine popped in front of Phoebe, and Claude rushed in front of Clementine.

The Forgettable took two steps back and held up a hand. "Whoa!"

"She's okay," Clementine said. "Just grabbing something for a friend and we'll be out of your way." She acted as if she wasn't in his house unannounced, as if the door hadn't been locked. (It hadn't been for her. Just for Claude.)

"You know where Jasper is? Is he okay?"

"I don't know a Jasper," Clementine's smile was easier than Phoebe's. Her history with the man was different. "Now, if you'll excuse us..."

Claude pushed forward and through the doorway, covering the walls and floor and ceiling, pushing the Forgettable back down the hall. Clementine popped her head out the door.

"I just have some questions—" the man said.

"No time," Clementine grabbed Phoebe's arm and pulled her out the door and walked briskly away. Phoebe looked back, but besides the spiders taking a ride on Clementine, Claude didn't follow.

"He knew me," Phoebe said. "And I think I knew him."

"You did."

"I don't remember. And I won't remember seeing him here."

"Neither of us will," Clementine added. "No worries. Claude will tell us all about it once we're far away."

Dr. Viel stood in the doorway. "Your greatest moment lies in that hospital tonight. You realize that, Gep?"

"Of course I do." Gep pushed at Viel, but Viel held strong.

"Gep, listen to me. Listen..."

Gep clenched his fist, ready to use it.

Viel smiled and laughed at what he was orchestrating. "Your greatest moment lies in that hospital. But you won't be there to see it. More importantly, the baby born in that hospital tonight will be as forgettable to you as the rest of the world. Just another face in the crowd...nothing more."

That was all Gep could stand to hear.

Viel didn't even see the punch coming, but he didn't care. He wiped his mouth, but the smile remained.

Gep scowled. "What are you doing, Viel? Why would you do this to me?"

"You try to take everything from me. That's not how this works, Gep." Viel pointed at his own chest. "I win this

*one. I get the scientific discovery. I get the girl. And you..."*
*Viel pointed at Gep's chest. "...you get to live in squalor,*
*knowing that at any moment I can choose my words oh so*
*carefully and watch you become... my... puppet."*

*"I have to get to my son." Gep's face grew hot and tears*
*began to form.*

*"You won't get there; it's too late. I've already said it.*
*You're abandoning your child, and his mother. I'll take it*
*from here." Dr. Viel stepped out of the doorway, walked*
*down the hall and out of the building, not even concerned*
*with if Gep could fight the words that had taken form.*

*Gep on the other hand, hoped. He stumbled out the*
*door, clambered into a car. Determined but clumsy,*
*shaken. So before he could even leave the parking lot, he*
*had crashed into the building. He laid his arms across the*
*steering wheel and let his face fall into them.*

*Shame enveloped him. He didn't go to the hospital that*
*night to see the lady who had chosen him, who had given*
*birth to their son.*

*He didn't meet the son. He didn't chase after the girl.*
*He just gave up as Dr. Viel's words took hold.*

# 31

HAT WAS QUICK," RaeCh says. She stands at the door with, dare I say, an impressed look on her face.

Clementine and Phoebe stand outside, Clementine holding up a handful of papers. A few spiders hover in Clementine's hair and neck, but the usual shroud is missing.

"Where's the rest?" I ask, peeking around the corner cautiously.

"These were all the notes we saw," Clementine says. Then, "Oh! You mean Claude. He'll catch up later."

"Kinda figured you didn't go anywhere without him," RaeChaeline says.

"He's here." Clementine smiles and holds out the papers to me.

I hesitate. We hadn't beat Ferg home last time, and I'd told myself it was a blessing in disguise. A clean break. I'd listened to myself, the boy in the notes, and I'd left it behind. And now they'd caught up to me again. I'd caught up to myself.

I reach out and take the notes. They're worse for wear, more crumpled than before, and water spots. "Did you read them?"

"Almost," Clementine says. "Phoebe reminded me of my manners. But I can't speak for Claude, he loves a good story."

156

RaeCh discreetly elbows me. *Claude* does *read*, it says, at least if elbows could talk.

"Don't we all," RaeCh says. "Come in."

We all walk to the sitting room, and, well, sit. I tap my foot. "What now?"

RaeChaeline is poised on the arm of a chair, probably to look down at her minions just ever so slightly. "How'd the mission go?"

"Uneventful," Clementine slumps back in boredom. The few spiders took a perch on the chair beside and above her. "Claude got all the action, kept the guy away."

"How convenient," RaeCh says.

"The guy?" I say. "You saw him?"

"Of course," Clementine says.

"How would you know?" RaeChaeline says. "It's not a dark memory?"

"Oh, it is. Claude told me, though."

"Again, convenient."

"So Claude remembers?" I ask. "He knows about this guy, I mean?"

RaeChaeline stands and walks over beside me, sits on the arm of my chair this time.

Clementine beams and pats a small spider with her fingertip oh so carefully. "Oh, yes. Claude has a great memory, and as I mentioned loves a good story. He collects them."

"What does he—"

RaeChaeline clamps a hand over my mouth. "Okay, enough of the interrogation, silly. They're clearly here to help."

Clementine nods.

RaeChaeline slowly lifts her hand off my mouth, one finger at a time as if she's not certain I took the hint. Understandable. Usually I don't.

"What now?" Phoebe asks.

"An excellent question," RaeChaeline says. "Now we here need some time for Max to write up some evidence. You can use that time to find out about Gep. Any news from Dr. Evil on bringing him back."

Clementine's face pinches in. She is probably about to ask why she is doing the grunt work. But before she does, she perks up. Lightbulb. "Oh, I'll have Claude check out all the material there. He'll get through that bookshelf before any of us could. Absolute genius." She stands, and Claude climbs down and onto her shoe.

Clementine practically prances out the door with Phoebe following. "You can keep an eye on her," RaeChaeline says.

"Of course," Phoebe agrees. "And read."

"Does any of it matter?" RaeChaeline asks.

Phoebe shrugs. "Does it ever?

# 32

LEMENTINE STRUCK A MATCH and lit the old lamp on
Dr. Evil's desk. It flickered and bounced its glow across
the shelves enticingly. But, in time...

Clementine picked up one of the books from Dr. Evil's desk,
flipped it open to its dog-eared page and began reading.

"What are we looking for?" Phoebe said.

"An answer to bringing a dead guy back to life. I said Claude
would read all the books in here, but joke's on me because of course
spiders can't read, so if I'm gonna keep up his ruse I gotta find
something that sounds snooty and academic."

"And you're only telling me this because I won't remember."

"Assuming I have some better decision to make in my life than
this, yep." Clementine turned a page and plopped into Dr. Evil's
desk.

Phoebe browsed the shelves again, for the hundredth time, all
the sights new and yet not. She brushed the books' spines with her
fingers. Claude began to crawl up the shelves and make himself
comfortable.

A bang startled Phoebe out of her search. Clementine had dropped the book on the floor and stood up. "Done! Did you know that the spider genome is similar to humans, with short exons and long introns?"

"You did not just find that in two pages of the first book."

"No, it's something Claude picked up in all these piles of books he reads tonight, and this is his favorite tidbit." Clementine smiled. "Come now. Let's find out what we can from Dr. Evil. I'm bored."

"What's that god-awful racket?" Dr. Evil stepped around the corner, his mustache quirking in disapproval.

"Right on schedule," Clementine said. "Any update on Gep?"

"Of course not," Dr. Evil said. "RaeChaeline is the answer, she just doesn't want to hear it."

"How is she the answer?" Phoebe asked.

Dr. Evil snapped his fingers. "Just like that she could bring him back if she wanted. Finds the right phrase and up he is, ready to terrorize us all over again."

"So you're saying RaeChae doesn't want him back?" Clementine quizzed.

"I would say no such thing." He picked up a page of scribbles on the table next to him and scrutinized it. "All the science in the world doesn't explain what we've done. She wants science as much as I do, though for opposite reasons. We both want something certain. She wants it to be certain her comrade will return. I want it to be certain that I can harness whatever is happening. And we both refuse to accept that there's a magic we can't control within it."

He passed the page to Phoebe, who looked at it then passed it to Clementine. Clementine held it up for Claude to see, too. "What are we looking at?"

"Just a distraction," Dr. Evil said. Clementine looked up. He stood at the front door, slammed it closed, and locked it. He held up the key and smiled, then walked away. Moments later, they heard his car drive away.

"There's gotta be another way out of here, right?" Phoebe said.

"For Claude, of course. He probably thought ahead about us, though."

"Ready for the kicker?"

"Bring it."

"That was the one memory I had of him."

"His most impactful decision. Hm." Clementine nodded. "Not bad."

# 33

**Y**OU THINK IT'S A DECISION in his favor or ours?"

Clementine climbed down the ladder from the attic. Her and Phoebe had scoured the building for an escape, but each window and door had been reinforced or jammed or otherwise rendered useless.

"I don't get to see that," Phoebe said. "I don't even technically know the whole 'most important' thing. That's just a shorthand reference for 'hey, these memories seem to be pretty big things usually.'"

"But not a climax."

"No, more like a catalyst. The first domino, the first rumblings of a stampede on its way."

"But we don't know if it's a stampede to trample us or a stampede of, like, lovable Claude." Clementine gestured at the spiders gathering.

"I guess. What we have doesn't come with a manual, right?"

"Tell me about it."

"Can those help?" Phoebe asked.

"Claude? Oh, he'll let us know if he finds a way. The lock is a conveniently Claude-proof variety Dr. Evil found through trial and error long ago."

Spiders were swarming the house, squeezing through every crack and filling every wall, even piling on top of each other. They only saved space for Phoebe and Clementine to move a couple of feet or so.

Phoebe picked up a bronze table lamp and swung it at the rickety back door. It made a thud. She swung again. A cracking sound, though upon inspection it left no dent.

"It's no use," Clementine said. "He would account for brute force. We have to think of something he wouldn't account for."

"Like what?" Phoebe dropped the lamp and walked past Clementine to open the door to Gep's room, the spiders clearing the doorknob just in time.

Gep's room was covered with spiders as well. Phoebe approached Gep, who was also covered in spiders. She reached out to touch him and a path cleared. "He's really dead."

"Very dead," Clementine responded. "Do you remember him, after…?"

Phoebe turned and leaned against the table, the spiders again hopping over each other to give her space. Phoebe didn't answer the question, and instead asked her own. "What did we come here for?"

Clementine shrugged. "Form an alliance by selling out the guy that locked us here, I guess. Hopefully get this guy to live again along the way."

"We have unparalleled access to this space. We can use that against him."

"What, like, investigate a locked attic to see what secrets he's hiding?"

"Exactly."

Clementine waved her hand in dismissal. "Sorry, inside joke. You already searched the attic."

Phoebe huffed and pursed her lips.

Clementine reached down and scooped up a handful of spiders. "We've been locked up before..."

"How did you escape?"

"Had an inside man. On the outside, I mean."

"Yes! On the outside. We just need someone out there."

Claude began to climb up Clementine's pants. Clementine nodded. "Claude is getting anxious. Something isn't right."

Phoebe looked around and sniffed, but noticed nothing amiss besides the spiders. They were piling even higher as more spilled into the building.

"He's trying to tell me something," Clementine said.

"Like what?"

Clementine shook her head and sat on the floor. "Anyhow, we're the inside man, so unless RaeChaeline pops by when she hasn't heard from us, we're on our own.

# 34

'VE WRITTEN FAKE NOTES that Fancy mostly approves of. There's some tweaks still, but I get a break today. Something about getting the pawns in place before locking in on one direction. One move at a time, keeping options open to see how the game plays out.

Oh, but by "break" I just mean from writing. My hand gets a break. I don't. We're going to re-attempt recruiting, I guess.

RaeChaeline wants to put on the heat, and who better to heat things up than the catalysts of this entire story, the dear and distressed Mr. and Mrs. Trencher.

So we leave the Trenchers' old home we'd been squatting in and head to the Trenchers' new home. The one with the creepy patchwork Julia sculpture. Now that I've met her, I see the resemblance.

RaeChaeline breezes into the space as if she owns it. She must have forgotten they're our benefactors and not the other way around.

Julia and the Trenchers are eating brunch at a lengthy table in awkward silence, just as you'd imagine.

"Don't mind me," RaeChaeline says as she sits in the open seat across from Julia.

I scoot into the seat next to RaeCh, ducking my head in apology.

"We need to change the locks," Mr. Trencher says.

"They don't have a key," Mrs. Trencher reminds him.

RaeChaeline scoops a handful of grapes onto the plate conveniently already set before her, and pops one in her mouth. "No need to change the locks if you just use them."

Julia shrugs. "Didn't realize there was a need."

"Aren't your living quarters across town more than adequate?" Mrs. Trencher asks.

RaeChaeline smiles and picks up another grape. "More, yes."

"It's lovely," I agree. She side-eyes me.

"Mr. and Mrs. Trencher," RaeChaeline segues into her prepared monologue. "I thought it apt to warn you that with the circus... resurrected per se..." (She pauses, not because she didn't know what would come next, but for dramatic effect, to appear unscripted.) "...the police have reopened the investigation and are snooping about."

"What's to investigate?" Mr. Trencher furrows his eyebrows.

"Yes, we have Julia here now." Mrs. Trencher reaches toward Julia, nearly clasping her hand before patting the table in her direction instead.

"Absolutely nothing to investigate," Julia pipes in.

"Nothing..." Mr. Trencher repeats.

RaeChaeline jumps in. "You may remember there are still... rumblings of missing persons besides our dear Julia."

"So dear," Julia mocks. She stands and pushes her chair in. "I won't listen to this. The circus is fine. I'm fine. Mr. and Mrs. Trencher are fine. We don't need to drudge this up."

RaeChaeline smiles with false innocence.

Julia grabs an orange and walks out the door. "Don't lock it, I'll be late!" she hollers behind her.

Since everyone else is eating, I figure I may as well too, and grab a cake square and finger sandwich.

Mrs. Trencher clears her throat. "Guess now's a good time to retire to the drawing room."

Mr. Trencher stands, and Mrs. Trencher follows suit. RaeChaeline smirks at me. I shove the cake square in my mouth and follow.

"They didn't know I was eating, you know," RaeCh whispers in my ear as we sit on a couch.

I smile as if I knew that, but I'm nowhere near as good an actor as she.

RaeCh turns back to Mr. and Mrs. Trencher. "There really is a solution where we can all walk away from this as if it never happened."

"Never happened," Mr. Trencher repeats.

Mrs. Trencher sniffs. "And how much will that solution cost?"

"How much?" I ask.

"You came to us for a reason."

"Believe it or not," RaeChaeline interjects, "money isn't the only thing you have."

"It's certainly the most notable."

"You have Julia's ear. It's tense, of course, but ultimately she knows you want what's best for her, right?"

"Naturally," Mrs. Trencher says with emphasis, as if she has a point to prove.

RaeChaeline smiles. Everything was set up perfectly. Now to nudge the first domino... "All you have to do is convince her to travel with the circus when they leave next week."

Mrs. Trencher gasps.

"It is critical she goes on tour with them for the last dregs of summer."

"Preposterous," Mrs. Trencher says.

Mr. Trencher nods.

RaeChaeline continues, "If she leaves with them, there's nothing left here to stir up. It all dies down. She returns mid-autumn and you're one happy family again."

"Then she leaves with us," Mr. Trencher suggests. "We take a family holiday."

It's Mrs. Trencher's turn to nod.

"That's not enough," RaeChaeline says. "Persons of interest leaving in different directions will seem suspect. We're trying to lay low here, and just happening that everyone goes on circus tour is much more convincing."

"I've heard enough." Mrs. Trencher stands. "I've lost enough to this circus. I won't lose more."

RaeChaeline and I stand in unison.

"I urge you to reconsider," RaeChaeline says as we head out. I sneak the finger sandwich in my pocket as we walk through the dining area. Then we're out. RaeChaeline snaps her finger and smiles as we turn the corner. We did it.

# 35

**W**HAT'S HIS PLAN FOR US, anyhow?" Phoebe asked.

They both sat on the floor in front of Gep, leaning back on the table. Claude had transitioned as well from his frantic swarming to a sort of settled state, slowly ebbing and flowing across the surfaces.

Clementine shrugged. "He's not like RaeChae. He doesn't have it all mapped out ten steps ahead. He just has, like, three steps maybe. He wanted us—me and Claude really, you're just collateral—locked up. He figured out enough for that, and now that we're trapped he'll figure out how to feed us or push us back to the attic or whatever he decides from here."

"Kill us?"

Clementine shook her head. "He wouldn't try that."

Phoebe sighed. "I can live with that."

"So could I."

# 36

HE THING ABOUT DOMINOS: They take a long time to set up. And if you're not careful, you knock one over and the chain takes off without the rest of the pieces. There's a lot of deliberation. A lot of particularity. A lot of patience.

Fancy would be the first to tell me I have none of those things, but lucky for me she has all of them.

We've got Phebe and spider girl doing our bidding, memorizing a bajillion dry textbooks to bring Gep to life.

We've got the Trenchers where we want them, which means soon we'll have Julia and the rest of the cirque folk where we want them. But the Trencher implosion and reading books takes time, time where our minions do our bidding and we have to just sit here and wait. So Fancy says.

She's off in her head, scheming I'm sure. Planning the ten steps after the ten steps she already has in place. Trying to bring the dead bird not-so-affectionately named Discovery back in order to bring Geppetto back. Planning her and Gep riding off into the sunset.

And here I am, stuck in my head, writing. Stuck on the one step after the ten steps she has planned. Where would I be riding off to, and more importantly who would I be riding with?

I have no clue.

I touch the notes from past me, from Jasper. I skim and try to remember something. But I keep pulling back out, not from the darkness that I had in place of memories, but from the warnings I had given myself. I was supposed to move on. And I was. I think.

I hadn't met the Ferg guy. I'd made my own life, or was making it at least. Sure, it was a mess, but it was mine.

Jasper would be proud of that. Right?

I didn't know. Because I didn't know him. I didn't know me.

Would he want a future with Ferg, now that he saw the mess I make of it on my own?

Would he want a future with Fancy 1.0 or Fancy 2.0? Not that they'd have me, probably, but the concept of a new companion was there.

Would Jasper want a future all his own? That's what I suspected most. There was this nagging feeling that I hadn't left him as far behind as I pretend. That there is a glimmer of him every time I look in a mirror, every time I took off on one of Fancy's schemes, every time I write here on this paper. He's secretly always there, and I just can't quite see him behind myself. And that's what scares me.

# 37

HE WALK WAS LONG, which you'd think would give Julia time to cool off. But no. Was she upset at RaeChaeline? At Analiese? At herself?

She wasn't sure. And she wasn't ready to confront that question, so instead she'd confront Analiese.

The Julia from before wouldn't let Mr. and Mrs. Trencher control her life—she'd escaped. The Julia from before wouldn't let Analiese push her away from the circus—she'd stayed.

Yet she wasn't the Julia from before anymore. She wasn't sure who she was, so she had resorted to letting others lead her any which way in the meantime.

But no more.

She banged on Analiese's wagon door. No matter that she was likely waking the night owl.

The door creaked open, and Analiese groggily peeked out. "Oh. You."

"I'm joining the circus."

Analiese cleared her throat. "Straight to the point, I see. Can I at least wake up before you make your demands? Or will you change your mind by then all over again?"

Julia put her hands on her hips and huffed. "What's *that* supposed to mean?"

"You're running away to the circus, then it scares you off, then back to the circus, back to mommy and daddy, then back, then away, and now here we are." Analiese peeked at the reflection in the window and raked her fingers through her hair.

"You told me I don't belong."

"And you believed me!"

Julia tapped her foot on the ground. "Look, Mr. and Mrs. Trencher are going on holiday, and..."

"Aww, poor you, a forced vacation."

"I have nowhere else to go, and RaeChae warned them—"

Analiese stopped studying her reflection and cut Julia off with a stern gaze. "RaeChaeline what?"

"Cops are circling, and she's sending us away."

"And they believed her?"

Julia shrugged.

Analiese shook her head. "They wouldn't."

Julia tucked her hair behind her ear. "Please. Let me stay. I'll learn to juggle or be a cook or stage hand or..."

Analiese smirked. "You're under the delusion you can take my old job?"

"I'll do anything."

"Not that. You'll change your mind is what you'll do." Analiese stepped out of the doorway and locked up. "Follow me."

# 38

E STILL HAVEN'T HEARD from Phoebe and Clementine. Not a single spider has been seen traversing the walls. It's eerie. And Fancy is beginning to wonder if she'd given her puppets too much leash.

But she didn't have time to worry about that, because when one domino collapses, so does the next, and the next, and the next.

We wake to banging at the door, and there stands a whole circus troupe. Or, the ones we know at least.

Analiese leads them in—of course, she lived here before any of us except Julia, and she was always more at home here than Julia ever was. They sprawl out in the drawing room like they own the place: Analiese, Nick, Julia, some guy named Sullivan.

"What's the plan?" Analiese asks.

RaeChaeline smiles triumphantly. "Knew you'd come around."

"Mr. and Mrs. Trencher don't trust you, and that pulled Julia in, and now we're a package deal I guess, so..."

"Ah, like the enemy of my enemy is my friend, only..." RaeChaeline touches her fingers to her mouth as she ponders "...the person distrusted by the person I distrust is someone I can—"

"We don't trust you," Analiese says. "We just might see eye to eye on this. *Might.* Depending on your next words."

"You seen Phoebe lately by chance?"

Analiese shakes her head. "Hasn't been by her wagon in a couple days. Should I be worried?"

"We should always be worried."

Analiese nods. "So what do we tell the cops?"

"It needs to be a cohesive message that gets the cops to look at Dr. Evil's place, but not so repetitive that it sounds like a cover."

I nod solemnly.

"Obviously." Analiese rolls her eyes.

"To ensure no mess-ups, I'll give each of you one piece of the story. Just the piece you supposedly witnessed. That way no one trips up."

"You think I'm falling for that?" Analiese says. "I know you have control issues, but we'll be more effective if we all know the plan so we can improvise in the correct direction. This isn't some script. We can't control what the cops will ask."

RaeChaeline sighs and looks out the window.

This was not her Plan A, but I'm sure she is pivoting to her Plan B as we speak. That's the thing with RaeChaeline. It doesn't matter if it's not the first script she's written in her head, because she's simultaneously written a nearly infinite number of scripts and could switch to them at will. You could think you were throwing her off when in fact she'd seen it coming three days ago, along with the ten other options you could have thrown her with, and she's accounted for each of them to go the direction she ultimately wants to land.

"RaeChae, we can help you," Nick says. "You had our back at the bonfire. We have your back. You just gotta trust us."

RaeChaeline's chin quivers, and I wonder if it's a ruse. I could never tell with her.

She turns back to the group. "Fine. We have Max's notes leading right to Dr. Evil as the suspect. We just need to get them to that building. Some of us need to be aware of him being the benefactor of the circus," RaeChaeline looks at Analiese. "Others need to be unawares." She looks at Julia. "It really comes down to the details. Having no info about the crimes to lead us on our own anywhere, but just enough of a mention of Dr. Evil to get the cops thinking maybe we missed something there."

The group falls silent, thinking.

Then, Analiese nods. "Makes sense. You got the scripts?"

RaeChaeline shakes her head. "You don't want scripts, you don't get scripts. But you screw this up, it'll all fall back on your little circus crew. Mark my words."

"We'll be out of your hair in no time," Analiese says. "Our show hits the road in a matter of days."

"Convenient timing," RaeChaeline says. "Max? We have notes to write before the search warrant hits." And with that she shoos everyone out, quite satisfied with that development but quite worried about the other pawns she has in play.

# 39

PHOEBE AND CLEMENTINE HAD WAITED, but Clementine was right. Something was different about being locked up this time. Dr. Evil wasn't coming. He would wait them out, let them starve. He wouldn't kill them, no, but he wouldn't keep them from dying, and that was acceptable enough to his conscience.

Claude carried crumbs in to share, but nothing substantial enough would fit through the cracks of the building to really help.

"We have to find food," Phoebe said. "It's been too long."

Clementine held up two fingers. "Just two days. But you're right." She stood and swayed.

"What's the plan?" Phoebe said.

"I don't know. RaeChaeline should be worried about us by now. But perhaps we're expendable."

Phoebe nodded and stood. "We could write a note for help. Send Claude."

"She won't listen to Claude without a bribe, something in it for her."

"Then who would?"

Clementine thought about it. And she didn't like the answer she came up with.

"You thought of someone," Phoebe said, recognizing the change in facial expression.

"It's a bad option."

"It's something…"

"You won't like it."

Phoebe stumbled to the countertop, picked up a pen and paper, and wrote.

"Sign your name," Clementine said. "The Forgettable will come to save you."

Phoebe paused. "You're right. I don't like the sound of that."

But they gave the note to Claude, and the spiders began to carry it away. Help would be on the way. Just not yet. "It will take most the day to get there," Clementine said. "Hopefully he's home."

"Then we got time," Phoebe said. "Tell me: Why do I not like this option?"

"Because he loves you," Clementine said.

Phoebe grew silent. "Oh."

"Not the good love, though. I mean, maybe some. But also the obsessive love. The love that sees you in the light of what you could be for them instead of who you actually are."

"Is there any different?"

"Of course. It's just rare." Clementine sat back down. "He was convinced he knew better than you, because you know…your memory. When he wanted to run off and you wanted to stay. Figured you didn't know yourself, know others. Didn't realize maybe he's the one that didn't know you."

"You were there?"

"Claude was. He loves a good story, especially a tragically fated romance."

"Just the sort of thing I love to star in."

"You're not the only one," Clementine assured. "This guy here, Gep. Thought he knew a girl, too. Dr. Evil and him both did. Figured they both knew her better than the other, and her story didn't matter except where it intersected with theirs. Fought over her 'til she was gone, but by then they'd forgotten what they were competing for and just kept going."

"RaeChaeline?"

Clementine shook her head. "Doesn't matter. Now we're just little puppets in the world they're building for themselves."

It was Phoebe's turn to shake her head. "That's what they think. But like you said, they don't see us. They see what they want to see, and that's their blind spot."

Clementine pondered, then smiled, a spark in her eye. "You're right. They just see a couple puppets put away in a toybox. They forget their most prized possession." She glanced at Gep's body. "We may not need lover boy's rescue after all."

# 40

E NEED TO FIND OUT what's up with the spiders and Phoebe." RaeCh paces. "It's too quiet."

She doesn't do well not knowing exactly where she stands with people.

I shrug. "It takes awhile for a human to read a bookshelf. And maybe it takes a spider even longer."

"It's not one spider. It's hundreds."

"Even still." I'm not quite sure how spider reading works, if they crawl across the page and can read as they go, or if they have to climb away from the page to read from a more human-like distance, then climb back down to turn the page, etc. etc. Either way, doesn't sound like a very efficient process. I'm still baffled it's even a thing, to be honest, but hey, I've learned this world has strange things.

"I will spend one more hour with Discovery, then we're off."

"Two," I suggest. "One for Discovery, one for a light lunch."

She breezes out to the back porch.

She's getting closer, I suspect. Closer to bringing Discovery back.

She would say it's impossible to know, that it's like a butterfly in a cocoon; it's either done or it's not, and if you try to peek ahead of time, you cut into the cocoon and the whole thing is dead. Oops. She would say you can't know until a beautiful butterfly bursts forth.

But I would say it's impossible to know a certain date or time, but very possible to tell. Firstly, you study one hundred other caterpillars that become butterflies and how long those take. A pattern emerges. And you know each day with this caterpillar, you're that much closer to being part of that pattern and having a butterfly break through. And I've had a front row seat to RaeChaeline's caterpillars for a bit. She doesn't accept caterpillars in her story for long.

She would have some snarky comeback about how I'm a caterpillar in her story, but that's why this is a conversation I imagine instead of actually have. I just smile and know we're getting closer and closer to the butterfly.

I begin to scour the pantry for the makings of a tasty meal.

# 41

RAECHAELINE HAD SPENT MANY LATE HOURS with Discovery. She wouldn't admit it to Max, but it wasn't a half bad idea. She'd tried hundreds or thousands of sentences to bring Discovery back to no avail. But it narrowed her options; like a lightbulb, she'd just found hundreds or thousands of ways to not bring Gep back. She just needed to find one that would.

And if today wouldn't be that day, one day would, and Gep would be waiting. She'd made sure of it.

If she'd learned one thing, it was patience.

So she grew quite fond of her time with Discovery, meticulously planning her words, and when they didn't bring Discovery back, it was a step forward nonetheless. She would lay across the bench for hours, looking up at the sky, imagining Discovery flying up there, and then saying something to make it so. And when Discovery continued to lay unmoving, she'd storm up a new sentence, or a tweak to the phrase, even just swapping out a word. Whatever it'd take.

Today she only had two hours. A little less, just enough to scarf down whatever atrocity Max cooked up.

She threw out one sentence after another, ones she'd been pondering in her conscious and subconscious all morning.

"Discovery will breathe again..."

"Discovery's heart will start..."

"Discovery will come to life..."

"...while I lay on this bench in peace."

"...today."

"...when I put my fingers on his chest."

Nothing.

Whatever magic in the universe wanted to mix or twist or take or give, it wasn't time.

Until it was.

As RaeChaeline was walking back into the house to eat, she paused at the door. Thought, then tried... "The dominos are falling into place for me. And Discovery coming back to life is one of those dominos. It's all coming together."

Then, finally, the domino fell.

Discovery twitched, his chest expanded, his wing fluttered.

RaeChaeline's eyes widened, her lips parted in awe. She peeked her head inside and called for Max.

She turned, and there was Discovery, perched on the back of the bench, chirping. RaeChaeline touched her hand to her chest and smiled.

Max opened the door behind her, and she gestured at Discovery. Discovery tilted his head, you would almost swear he smiled, then he flew away. Max hugged RaeChaeline before he realized, but RaeCh didn't even mind. She laughed and patted his back. He grabbed her hands and jumped in a circle in an awkward dance. *It's all coming together.*

# 42

E'S COMING!" Phoebe was looking out the window. Dr. Evil drove past, parking in front of his home. He was back.

"'Bout time," Clementine said.

"What now?"

"Now, we have our outside man, and our inside man."

"Dr. Evil?"

Clementine smiled. "He's not inside. Gep is." She sat in Dr. Evil's office chair. She opened the desk drawer and pulled out the matches.

Phoebe's stomach flip flopped. "You don't mean..."

"He might let us go, but he won't leave Gep."

Clementine struck the match, then lit the oil lamp. She blew out the match, picked up the lamp, and stood.

"Get ready..." Clementine dropped the lamp next to the bookcase. It shattered. "Oops."

The spiders scurried away, and Clementine grabbed Phoebe's hand and pulled her back down the hall toward Gep.

"Remember to breathe and stay low," Clementine said. "And stick with Gep. He's our ticket out of here."

Clementine took his arms, and Phoebe his legs. They lifted, and somewhat gingerly (as gingerly as one could with the weight of a dead, frozen body in such an urgent situation) dropped him on the floor as Claude cleared a path.

"Which way?" Phoebe asked.

"I don't know where he'll let us out. Let's try the front room. Most conspicuous."

They stumbled out of the hallway and into the entryway that was filling with smoke. The books and shelf were in flames, as well as the desk. Phoebe led them to beneath the window and banged on it.

The spiders were back to a frenzied dance.

"No..." They heard Dr. Evil muffled outside. "No, no. What did you do!?"

"Let us out!" Clementine said.

"Where's Gep?" Dr. Evil found the window and peeked in.

"Here." Phoebe coughed.

Dr. Evil touched the glass, but quickly pulled away from the heat.

"You can save him," Clementine said. "We can save him."

Dr. Evil wasn't exactly resourceful in terms of putting out a fire, though. He hadn't planned an escape from the building. He had figured there'd be time to eventually get in and do what must be done. "G-go to the back," he said. "That's our best chance."

Clementine and Phoebe and Claude crawled to the hallway, the fire nearly beating them there.

Dr. Evil ran around the building. "Hang in there, Gep."

While those inside made their way to the back, Dr. Evil was prying and banging and trying to get the back door cleared. (Banging helped absolutely nothing at this point, but he wasn't in the most rational frame of mind.)

"Go quicker," Phoebe called to Clementine. "The fire..."

"I'm hurrying," Clementine called back.

But the fire was catching up, and Claude had begun to crawl on top of Phoebe, on top of Gep, on top of Clementine, wherever he could fit.

Phoebe coughed.

"Phoebe, we have to leave him," Clementine said. "Get up here."

Phoebe shook her head and coughed again. This was too familiar.

But the fire lapped at her feet, so she crawled in front of Gep.

"Let's go," Clementine said.

Claude began to spill out of the cracks of the back door first.

Something about this nagged at Phoebe. The corpse, the fire...her body knew this scenario. She didn't have the energy to argue, but she wouldn't leave Gep.

Phoebe grabbed his arm and pulled. Clementine saw and grabbed beneath Gep's other arm and pulled with her. They got to the end of the hall. Claude was making his way through the cracks, but that wasn't enough.

"Come on," Clementine said. "We need air."

"We have Gep," Phoebe added.

Claude crawled up Phoebe and Clementine's face, clambering for a quicker way out that didn't yet exist.

Dr. Evil had found an axe in the shed, and was hacking away.

The Forgettable ran up and pushed Dr. Evil away, and grabbed the axe from him. "Get something else."

The Forgettable began chopping.

Dr. Evil ran back to the shed.

RaeChaeline and Max arrived just behind the Forgettable.

"No!" RaeChaeline said.

The Forgettable got a hole in the doorway, and Claude came spilling out in waves.

Phoebe and Clementine gasped the air in. But so did the flames.

The Forgettable made another crack, and they all clambered to pull the wood from the door, to grab past the spiders to their people.

Clementine crawled out and stumbled past them. No one knew her enough to gasp in relief, to cry, to hold her tight. Claude surrounded her in a circle as she collapsed on the grass.

The Forgettable pulled Phoebe out and held her tight. She clung to him, too, and gasped in the air.

RaeChaeline and Dr. Evil grabbed Gep and pulled, but the fire had already taken his legs, his torso, and was making its way to his face.

"No!" RaeChaeline screamed. Max grabbed her and pulled her back, but she clawed at him.

Dr. Evil sat back as the fire took the rest of Gep, tears lighting up his eyes.

"Whyy..." RaeChaeline mumbled. "It can't..."

The Forgettable yelled, "Come on, everyone get back. It's not safe here."

Dr. Evil stumbled away. Claude and Clementine crawled. The Forgettable led Phoebe away. Max pulled at RaeChaeline.

They all watched as the fire took the building, took Gep, took their aspirations and hopes. The things that each of them clung to. They said goodbye to a competitor, a father, a companion. They watched as the fire was put out, as the cops arrived, as the plan that RaeChaeline hadn't orchestrated occurred instead.

RaeCh mumbled something into Max's shirt that he couldn't quite hear. He ducked his head. "What'd you say?"

"Gep coming back to life is one of those dominos," he hears.

"It's not," he said. "Not anymore."

"It's all coming...together." It came out more like a plea than a fact.

# 43

HERE IT IS IN FRONT OF ME. Ashes that used to be books. Notes. The remnants of a lifetime of research.

And I realize...these notes I've been taking could go up in smoke like that one day, too.

Just moments ago I would have said you have to write everything down so you don't lose it. Now I'm realizing you can lose that, too. My hands twitch. Perhaps worrying they may be useless to me soon.

RaeChaeline screams as she touches Gep's charred face.

The pain must be too much to hold in.

"The dominos..." she sobs.

The realization that she killed her friend.

"They're still..."

Not just a temporary killing this time.

"It's all coming together."

It's now more final.

There is no going back.

"Sir." It's that cop lady in front of me. Jenkins.

I inhale. I haven't been instructed by RaeCh how to respond. She hasn't planned for this.

"May I ask what you were doing here?" Jenkins asks.

I lick my lips. Am I allowed to say no to that question? "Sure," I croak out.

She touches my arm, almost sympathetic. "Tell me...What brought you here?"

I don't know how to think on my feet. I try to imagine RaeCh, whispering in my ear a backup plan. But all I can hear is that scream. All I can think about is Evil's notes gone. "M-my notes..." I stumble.

"Were you investigating here?"

I remember RaeCh wanted Dr. Evil to go down for this. Or Clementine. She hadn't made up her mind, I don't think. And the dead body was the wrong one, but the rest kind of lined up. "I guess."

I look around, taking in the scene. Dr. Evil is talking to the cops, probably spinning his story. Clementine lays in the grass, breathing deeply. Spiders sit on her stomach and around her, riding up and down, up and down, with each breath she takes, basking in the feeling that she indeed is still alive. Maybe no one wants to approach her considering all her...friends. The Forgettable and Phoebe are nowhere to be seen. RaeChaeline kneels next to the burnt body still.

It's entirely up to me to make sure the blame falls in the right hands, and I'm pretty sure that is Dr. Evil's hands, but what do I know.

"I... I have the notes," I muster. "I can bring them by. To help."

Jenkins nods. "I need to know what happened here."

"I just arrived as it was happening," I say truthfully. "I'm not sure."

"What did you see?"

I point at Dr. Evil. "He was trying to get into the building, and there was smoke coming out of it everywhere."

"And when he did...? Get in?" she prods.

"The body caught on fire," I whisper. I don't know if I'm supposed to say this. If it's part of the spin RaeCh would want.

"It was already dead," a voice behind me pipes in. Clementine. She appears next to me, the spiders staying at a distance. "The body there."

"It's been dead awhile," Jenkins adds.

Clementine nods.

"And you are?"

"Clementine Viel." She reaches out and shakes Jenkins' hand then brushes her hair out of her face. Almost composed. I note a movement in her hair and see a spider, hiding. Further in.

"Where were you?" the cop asks her.

"I was in the building. Found the body and crawled out with it. I got stuck, and Dr. Viel helped."

"And how were you stuck?"

Clementine shrugs. "You'd have to ask him."

Jenkins nods. Furrows her brows. She's considering something, and I wonder what we'd divulged. "Either of you know a Jasper, by chance?"

My breath quickens. I thought I had plenty of adrenaline already, but this was a new kick. She knew something. Was it the vomit in the field? Was it evidence I left somewhere that incriminated me somehow?

Clementine shakes her head. "No idea."

Jenkins nods then looks at me.

"Jasper?" I squeak.

Jenkins nods again.

I'm not being convincing. "Could be anybody, I suppose." Worst answer ever.

"Sooo, no? Or yes?"

I shake my head.

She scratches something on her paper and rolls her eyes. I guess that's sufficient for now, at least.

We continue to be questioned by the cops—not about Jasper but about the fire—and prodded by the medics, but finally we are left alone. And then Clementine pulls me aside. "What's the game plan now?"

"I thought you knew," I say.

"I'll tell you one thing. Your mastermind doesn't have a plan, and Dr. Evil does, so if you don't want this all to fall right back on us we need a solution now."

I nod. "Sounds like we need another clandestine rendezvous."

RaeChaeline leans against me, and I wrap my arm around her. She's become a shadow of what she had been, all the strength and confidence fading to frailty so quickly.

Clementine and Claude follow. As we stumble away, both emotionally and physically exhausted, we come across them. Phoebe and Ferg. I don't even notice until we're on top of them, or I may have found a detour. But now I'll never know.

They had been sitting under a tree across the street and a couple blocks down. Waiting.

"Jasper," the man says. The name is full of recognition, familiarity that I don't reciprocate.

Clementine rushes ahead and hugs Phoebe, holding her tight. Claude welcomes her, too, the spiders crawling from Clementine to Phoebe.

I look at the man, the oh so Forgettable, trying to conjure a memory, a feeling, something. "I'm Max now."

The Forgettable looks back, studying, realizing... "You don't remember either."

I shake my head.

RaeChaeline looks Ferg up and down disapprovingly. "You're the wrong corpse."

"Be nice," I whisper, as if she *could* be even on a good day. Then to Ferg, I say, "Look, I know... I know we had some sort of life together. I just don't remember what it was..."

"I get it. I'm complicated," he says, surely not getting it. Probably judging me for being too afraid to reconnect with my past life. "As long as you're safe. I'm here if you need me."

I nod.

He hands me a pen and paper. "Write it down. Now. You won't remember this when I leave."

So I do, then he does. And the memory fades to black.

Phoebe, Clementine, and Claude part ways with us. They go to the circus, and RaeCh and I head home.

She glances at the mirror in the entryway, then looks at the floor. Jasper looks back from the mirror too, frowning. I ignore him and lead RaeCh to a couch, and she falls asleep. Then I do, too.

**44**

LAUDE GOT THE INVITES OUT this time. With Clementine planning this one, it was a little more open invitation. For one thing, Sylas would be invited, and...well...

Clementine resigned herself to the one invite that deserved a hand delivery. She wrapped the extra gift in a box and stuck a quick note on top.

Minutes later, she looked at the door before her. A lump of emotion got stuck in her throat. She sniffed, took a deep breath, stroked her hair for Claude's reassurance. Then knocked.

The wait stretched longer than her years in the attic, and her legs grew weak; yet only a moment later the door creaked open.

Ferg peeked his head out between the crack. "Can I help you?"

Was it gruff? Matter of fact? She couldn't tell. "Do you remember me?" she squeaked out.

"You remember?" He opened the door further and leaned against the door frame. "The fire, or the break-in?"

Clementine frowned. "It wasn't a br-" She cut herself off. *Not the point.* "You don't remember...before?"

Ferg tapped the door frame with his fingers. "I'm not the one to forget."

Clementine felt Claude creeping along her arm. A warning. Something was off. She turned away to clear her throat and looked around. No cops or bystanders. No Dr. Evil lurking.

Claude wasn't warning about others. He was warning about something closer. Here.

She glanced back at Ferg and smiled innocently. "Just wondering if you remember anything before the circus, ya know? All the darkness lurking around it—gotta be something on the other side?"

A shadow darkened his eyes. "I try not to remember back then. You'll have to ask someone else."

Clementine waved her hand dismissively. "Oh, sure. Can do."

*Not ready,* Claude told her. She bobbed her head in agreement.

Ferg just stood there, looking into the distance. The dark shadow, the dark memories, were too near.

Clementine cleared her throat and held out the gift. "Anyhow, this is for you. We'll be on our way."

Ferg didn't acknowledge, didn't hear.

Clementine lifted his hand and set the box in it. He stood straight, grasped the gift and studied it.

A box with a note on top that said "better range than you I think."

He looked back up.

Was it to ask about the gift? To thank her? To ask her to stay?

He didn't have time to decide. She and her spiders were already gone.

He opened the box and found an invite to meet at the circus grounds with the others later. And beneath that, the gift: a two-way radio.

# 45

AECHAELINE NEARLY DIDN'T COME. Why would she do anything now, let alone this? Why would she face all these people for judgment? What was she going for?

"Me," Max said. "You're going for me."

And, surprisingly, she did.

Ferg stood outside the circus grounds, listening through the device. Sylas entered ahead of Max and RaeCh. He looked up at the tent and began studying each spider, one by one.

"What happened?" Analiese asked the question that was on everyone's mind—at least, everyone who hadn't witnessed it.

"There was a fire," Clementine said, speaking into her own walkie so Ferg could hear as well. "No, that's... Dr. Evil locked us up. We started a fire to escape. And the cops found a body."

"...Gep," Analiese surmised.

"Here's the thing," Clementine said. "All that is beside the point."

Max leaned in. How could that be beside the point? Wasn't that what they all were after, some way to get out of this whole murder thing and do something about Gep in the meantime? (Sure, there was disagreement on what to do with him, but still...)

"We can't deny we've all been crafted to the whims of what most suits others. Puppets in their little game. We're either too extraordinary or not extraordinary enough, borne into their expectations of how we fit and don't fit into their lives."

"What's new," Analiese said.

"Exactly!" Clementine clapped. "The trajectory continues, and we all know where that lands us. Tied up... locked up... abandoned... Doing the little puppet dance to make it another day."

"That's not what this circus is," Analiese pushed back.

"I'm not talking about this circus," Clementine said. "This circus won't last in the world that's coming."

"And what is coming?"

"One or more of us being the fall guy for the deaths, the fires...all of them off scot-free while we rot."

"This sounds eerily familiar," Max whispered to RaeChaeline.

Clementine looked right at Max. "We have to stop competing with each other. We're no one's puppets. We have to climb out of their toybox and live our lives."

Max raised his hand.

Clementine nodded her head.

"Isn't that what we're doing?" Max said. "You're out of Dr. Evil's lair, Analiese started a new circus, RaeCh and I —"

"That's a start," Clementine acknowledged. "But that's still their toybox. The question is, what's your toybox?"

Max opened his mouth to answer, then closed his mouth again. He didn't know.

Clementine smiled and turned to the others. "I dare say only Analiese has found her toybox, and if we don't find ours then hers might be taken as well."

"And what's your toybox?" Phoebe asked.

Claude crept forward a couple inches, as if leaning in to hear.

"I have yet to find mine as well. And I'd like to finally have that chance."

"So what are you asking of us?" Analiese said. "Why did you call this meeting, besides offering a riveting monologue?"

"Same as RaeChaeline a week ago. We need a fall guy before we become one."

"And we're all on board with that..."

"Circumstances have changed. It's not as cold a case as yesterday."

"Thanks to you!" That was RaeChaeline.

For the first time, Clementine faltered, mouth half open and nothing coming out.

"It's not as cold a case because you lit it up," RaeChaeline spat. "It was all orchestrated perfectly, and you ruined it."

Clementine's eyes glistened. "I didn't mean to..."

"You killed him!"

Max grabbed onto RaeChaeline to hold her back. She struggled against him, but had lost most her fight.

"There are some things you can't come back from," Clementine said. "Even us."

Analiese jumped in. "Let's get some sleep. In the morning we can tackle this. Together."

*The difference is spreading. At first it was a drip here, another there. The magic they'd uncovered leaking out.*

*They weren't ready for the flood.*

*A stray word here, another there. It was just a conversation. Saying something nonchalant about Gep. That's what everyone thought, just as you might think of anyone you happen to converse with or about. Why would this be any different?*

*But see, that passerby across the way. Watch the offhand comment bounce from Gep to her without a thought, becoming her reality in an instant no one could control.*

*Look, that stranger handing RaeChaeline her cup of coffee. So oblivious to the silly quip that reaches out and grips him in its clutches.*

*They never see each other again, most of the time. It was just a brush of an encounter, if that. They never put together where it came from, this collateral damage, how it settled on them and directed their path. How could they?*

*It was just another person on the street, another forgettable face in the crowd. How could that conversation change anything?*

*And yet, piece by piece, year by year, word by word, the circus was being formed.*

# 46

**HAT'S YOUR TOYBOX?** I hear Clementine say again. Not for real. In my head. *What's your toybox?*

I'm all for extended metaphors, but I don't know the answer to that question. That's what I've been wondering. I think.

I can't worry about that now. I have to put it aside. I still got the threat of a search warrant hanging over me. I still got half a plan in action that I'm not sure if or how I'm supposed to deviate. And the master of plans is out of commission.

So I make breakfast. I coax RaeCh into eating two bites. (She says the food is crap, but it never stopped her from eating my cooking before.) And I drag her to the circus.

Her "toybox" as Clementine called it was Gep and some competition- ambition-dream thing. I didn't quite understand it, but I did understand that her toybox had been blown to smithereens, so this was a touchy subject.

We're the last ones there. Which makes sense considering the morning is almost over. They're all sitting, talking in muted tones. Clementine still holds the radio for Ferg.

"So what's the plan?" RaeChaeline says.

Clementine opens her mouth, but Analiese cuts in first. "Dr. Evil is the fall guy, just like you wanted."

RaeChaeline lets out a dry laugh. "Just like I wanted."

"That part," Analiese clarifies. "That piece is just like you wanted. Max has the notes that point that direction, right?"

I nod.

"Little louder for the people in the back." Clementine holds the radio up to my face.

"Yeah," I say.

"So the heat's a bit higher now," Analiese says. "And the collateral is...worse than planned...but we don't need to change anything."

RaeChaeline looks at the floor and nods. "Nothing needs to change. My plan is still on."

"I don't care if there are ten of us or ten million," Clementine adds. "I just want us to have our own lives. Speaking of..." She tosses me the radio.

I fumble with it like a hot potato, and it hits the ground.

"If you want to reconnect with Jasper without losing more..." Clementine shrugs. "Ferg says no pressure."

RaeCh picks it up and puts it in my hand, holding it firmly there until I grasp it. "I need a nap," she says. "Let's get outta here."

"Should I turn my notes in early?" I ask. "Without a warrant?"

Clementine reaches out and pushes the button on the radio in my hand. I'd forgotten.

I repeat into the radio: "Should I turn in the notes without a warrant?"

"Great thinking," Phoebe says.

"Earlier the better," Clementine adds, then releases the radio button.

And we leave, barely there even ten minutes. But it was probably good to get RaeCh out of the house.

We arrive home, and she gets antsy again. Pacing. On edge. I try to sit her down, but she's not one to take orders. She pushes me away, screams. I hold up my hands and stand back, but that's not enough.

She takes a fist and marches to the entryway, looking for something to take her anger out on. Her fist finds the mirror. She shatters it, but it shatters her, too.

I tentatively approach from behind. "You're bleeding." She lifts her hand to her face, and sure enough there's blood dripping down her arm, splashing like tears onto the fragments on the floor.

She shoves past me, a handprint of blood marking my sleeve. I'm no help here.

She locks herself in the bathroom, and I hear a crash, but before I have time to worry about that the faucet turns on. Clumsily cleaning the wound herself, I presume. I wait outside, asking to help, but she's not good at taking help.

After awhile, I sit on the floor outside, waiting. I could clean up the mess in the entry, but I'm not sure I should leave her like this.

Eventually she opens the door. Her hand is bandaged fairly well. I glance behind her and see the mirror above the sink is shattered as well.

I sigh. "I'll get a broom."

"Careful with your hands," she says. "They've been through enough."

I remember the day we first met. Her hand now matches what she'd done to mine, and I remember again how dangerous she is.

RaeChaeline has a tired energy after the meeting, after the tirade, after losing her everything. She paces outside, looking up at the sky...looking for Discovery, for Gep's angel, for a higher being?

I crack the window and watch her for a time from inside, worried, wondering.

"Everything is falling into place," she mutters over and over.

Then, she comes back in. "You can stop peeping. I'm fine."

"No you're not."

"Careful with your words."

I sigh. "I know this is difficult for...Fancy. The pain, the guilt..."

"Guilt? What guilt?"

"For, ya know..." I don't know if I can say it, should say it. I don't know what it could make her do. "...killing Gep."

She bangs her fist on the counter. "I didn't kill Gep. That thing did."

"Thing?"

"The spidery creature who has the audacity to consider herself human."

"Clementine."

RaeCh points at me. "Don't give her the dignity."

"He was already dead, RaeCh."

She glares at me, then looks away, shaking her head. "No, it was temporary, he was—"

"Dead. He was gone."

"I was bringing him back."

"There's some things you can't come back from."

RaeChaeline's breath catches. "You don't know what you're talking about."

I collect the notes we'd crafted together, the fake story for the cops. I place them in order, re-read them to make sure everything is there.

As I head to the door, RaeCh stops me. "Where are you going?"

"Taking these to the cops. Earlier the better."

"Wait, they're not right," she says.

"Oh," I say. "I didn't notice anything. What'd I miss?"

"Things have changed."

"But we're going with your plan."

"And the dominos didn't fall where we planned, so we need to adjust the story."

I sit at the table, and RaeCh sits next to me. She shows me what's wrong. The gaping hole in the story.

You see, I'd forgotten her plan.

Oh, I knew the plan everyone else knew. The plan they intended when they said her plan was on.

But at Psych Institute, RaeCh had confided in me a separate, secret plan. A plan with a different fall guy. And we'd told RaeCh that nothing had changed. The only thing that had changed really was RaeChaeline's resolve, as this morphed from a collateral situation to a story of revenge. Revenge against the person who wasn't part of the story earlier and had inserted herself since. The person who must now pay for the wrongs they've done to RaeCh.

Clementine.

# 47

AECH IS NAPPING. OR SOMETHING. She never napped before, so either the grief has zapped all her energy or she just needs time alone to cry or scheme or something. Or all of the above.

I'm supposed to be editing my notes for her review when she wakes.

Instead I stare at the cursed object on my nightstand. From a practical perspective, it could either get me out of this mess or further in. And sure, I'd like to wrestle with that decision a bit, but I'm too busy wrestling with if I'm ready to have my past meet my present.

I pick up the radio and push the button. Then my throat catches. I release the button, and set it down.

I leave the house and take a walk.

When I return, she's up. "I don't see any edits." She sits at the table scrutinizing my work, or lack thereof in this case.

"No, I was thinking about that, and then realized..." I gulp. "W-we can't rewrite this now," I try the practical approach. "It'll be suspect if I don't turn this in early like we all agreed."

RaeChaeline put her head in her hands. "What would you do that for!?"

"It made sense..."

"You don't move up the timeline!" she bangs the table.

"I didn't know that."

"Well then, we better hurry," RaeCh says. "You could have had this done by now."

RaeCh has me rewrite a touch here and there. Just enough to allude to Clementine being there without me supposedly knowing that Clementine was there sorta thing.

"This is a bad idea," I say.

"You wouldn't know a bad idea if it hit you in the face. Let alone a good one."

"How do we point to Clementine instead of Dr. Evil?" Again, I take the practical approach.

"We kill Dr. Evil," she counters. "Then there's only Clementine in that house to blame."

I nod. That could work. Crap.

The practical approach wasn't gonna get us anywhere. "Clementine is trying to help us," I try. "Why would we want her to be the fall guy?"

"She killed Gep." She's matter of fact. Immovable.

"Some might beg to differ."

RaeCh stands out of her seat and leans her hands on the table emphatically. "That's beside the point."

"No, that is the entire point," I yell back.

"Leave the thinking to me, will ya?"

I take a deep breath. Escalating isn't working. I try again, softly. "You're not in the best state of mind for that."

Her shoulders soften, and she regains her composure. "Who's fault is that?" she asks. "Clementine's."

I couldn't argue with that. While Clementine didn't kill Gep, she certainly is the reason RaeCh went from some endlessly meticulous, patient mastermind to a volatile bomb waiting to go off. I was hoping that just as one domino had pushed RaeCh this way, perhaps if I could find the right domino it could push RaeCh back over to where she had been.

But, that's not how grief works. There are some things that cannot be undone.

Stacking the odds in one person's favor naturally is stacking the odds against another, and RaeCh had played that game for too long to not be bitten back.

I don't want to broach the topic of having to kill Dr. Evil right now. Knowing that the previous RaeCh would kill in a heartbeat if it got what she wanted, I had no doubt that this RaeCh was okay with killing, too. So I'd leave that for another day.

Again, the practical approach. (Why do I suddenly have to be the practical one?) "What about Claude? I thought he was gonna get Clementine out of anything."

"You're right," RaeChaeline says, coming to her senses. She taps her fingers on the table and purses her lips. "Hmm... We'll have to find a way to incapacitate him, too."

That whole coming to her senses thing I mentioned...yeah...or not.

"I'll think on it," she adds.

Exasperated I say, "Guess you can use Discovery to test that out, too."

"Don't be heartless," she says. "We don't kill without reason."

RaeCh is delivering the fake notes to the cops. She wouldn't trust me with it.

I'm not sure when I'll next get a chance. Maybe it's not the right move, but it's a move.

I pick up the radio and let out a shiver. "Hello," I say.

Silence.

I sit down the radio and let out a breath.

"Jasper?" a voice comes from the other side.

My face grows hot as I pick up the radio. "Max," I correct.

"Oh, right. Max," he tries out. "Hi."

"I'm in kind of a bind," I say. Straight to the point.

"What's that?"

I stop. How do I say this? What do I divulge? How much should I give away? I decide: "I don't think Dr. Evil is gonna be the fall guy."

"...oh."

I wait. Should I say something else? What else should I say?

"What are you going to do?" he finally asks.

Fair question. What am I going to do? "...freak out."

He laughs. "You'll figure it out."

"What would Jasper have done?"

This time he's the one who leaves me waiting. "You should talk to Phoebe."

"About Jasper?"

"She doesn't know Jasper," he says. "But you do. And you should talk to her about that."

I don't see how talking to Phoebe, who won't even remember we had a conversation, will help me outsmart RaeChaeline or Clementine or whoever I'm supposed to be outsmarting. But it's what Ferg suggests, so that's something at least.

"Thank you," I say, with a touch of a question mark in my voice.

"It's nice talking to you again. Max."

"Err, same...maybe..."

"I'm glad you've made your own life."

I shake my head. "Am making. Maybe."

There's a pause. Then, with what sounds like a catch in his voice, "You deserve it, though."

He clears his throat, and I realize something is caught in mine as well. A forgotten memory, perhaps.

"Another time, then," he says.

"Yeah." I set the radio down and look around the room for evidence of the life I was making.

# 48

RUSH OUT OF THE HOUSE before RaeCh can catch me or before I lose my nerve.

I tiptoe through the circus as if I'm sneaking. Of course, I'm not actually sneaking, so I'm spotted by Nick and Julia.

"Hey," Julia says. "How's RaeChaeline?"

Straight to RaeCh, no concern for the person in front of her. "I'm fine, thank you," I muster dryly.

"Oh. Right."

"What Julia means is, well..." Nick stumbles over his words, and I realize I like this guy. "...we know she was close to Gep."

"Right," I say.

I want to say *She's conspiring to take Clementine down and kill Dr. Evil, and I don't know how to stop her or if I should*, but I'm not sure how.

Instead I say, "She's coming around."

Julia nods. "Maybe we all will."

"Maybe," I agree.

"My loss is different," Julia says.

"Of course," I say, not quite sure what her loss was. Is. Was she close to Gep?

"I still don't know if or how I'll recover, and it's been months."

Right. Months. "I don't think we're meant to recover," I say.

"Maybe," she agrees.

I clear my throat. "I'm looking for Phoebe."

Julia points me to Phoebe's circus wagon where I guess she lives. I approach, knock, wipe my sweaty hands on my pants. I look back, but Julia and Nick have moved on.

The door opens. Phoebe catches her breath when she sees me, touches her hand to her chest, then forces her breathing to slow. She lets me in and shows me a seat.

"I don't know if you remember me," I say. "I'm Max."

Phoebe brings me a cup of coffee and takes a sip of her own. "I remember some."

"Ferg sent me."

Phoebe smiles. "I'll pretend I know who that is."

"Right, uhh...some guy." I wave my hand in dismissal. "I'm worried about something that's about to happen maybe. And I don't know what I should do. I think maybe he sent me here because, ya know, maybe you'll see something. Or maybe you won't remember our conversation so I can uhh...get advice without changing things? Or something?"

Phoebe squints and takes a sip of her coffee.

I pick up mine and take a gulp. It's better than what I make.

"I'm hardly a fortune teller, but I'm certainly no psychologist," Phoebe says.

I blush and stand to leave. "Sorry."

"No doctor-patient confidentiality here," she clarifies.

"Oh, sure," I say. "I don't know what I meant by that. Just thinking out loud…"

She points back at my seat, and I sit again.

"With that in mind," Phoebe continues. "Do tell me whatever I'm not supposed to remember. My pride may be insulted, but my interest is piqued."

I ponder where to start, how to sum up so much that has happened, is happening. I take another gulp of coffee. "So, there's these dead guys. Or, guy, I guess now. And the cops are investigating."

Phoebe nods as if that all makes sense, so with a shot of confidence I continue.

"We're all suspects or people of interest or whatever."

"We?" she asks.

"The circus people and me and… Doesn't matter. We think Dr. Evil should be the fall guy. I mean, his nickname is Dr. Evil for a reason."

"What's that?"

I pause. "Not sure…"

Phoebe nods as if that makes sense. "Continue."

"You sure you're not a psychologist?" I ask.

Phoebe raises her brows and smiles.

When she doesn't answer, I continue. "Anyhow, RaeCh has her own plans to take out Clementine instead." I hold the mug up to my face, inhaling the warmth to catch my breath, gather my wits.

"And you're caught in the middle?"

I nod.

She reaches out and touches my hand. "And who do you think should take the fall?"

I tilt my head. What do I think? "Does it matter?" I ask.

"Shouldn't it?"

I lift my hand from hers to tap the handle of my mug. "I don't know what I think anymore."

"How come?"

I shrug. "I was someone else, before...something. But I don't remember. How can I trust myself when I don't even know who that is?"

Phoebe sets down her cup. "Now we're getting somewhere."

"Are we?"

"Your friend...Ferg?" she asks.

"I don't know if he's a friend..."

Phoebe nods. "He didn't send you here to side with RaeChae or Clementine. He sent you to help you side with someone else."

"Who?" I ask.

"Yourself."

I frown. *"Now* you're sounding like a psychologist."

"You don't trust yourself because you don't remember," Phoebe says.

"I think I made that clear."

"What would it take to trust yourself?" she asks.

I think about it. Two roads diverging, myself confidently walking down one, certain in my choice because I know who I am.

"RaeChaeline..." I bite my lip. "...she is meticulous. She plans out every step, every possible scenario, and then she just always knows which way she'll go. She knows what she wants and how to get there, because she knows who she is and how she would respond in every situation."

"Hmm."

"If I knew who I was, I could do that, be that. I could say in any situation 'I go this way. That's who I am. That's what I want.'"

Phoebe looks off into the distance and purses her lips.

"What do you think?" I ask.

"I think you hang out with planners too much," she says. "You're not RaeChaeline. You think you won't know yourself unless you can plan for every possibility, calculate every angle based on your history and future projections? That's not you. That's not Max. You have to stop wishing you were RaeChaeline and start being Max."

I lean back in my chair. "How do I...?"

"You may not have the memories," she says. "But your body knows. You still know who you are. And you get to decide every day who you are." Phoebe furrows her brows momentarily, considering something. Then smiles and says, "I don't remember most things either. But I still know. And you do, too. Stop trying to plan for every scenario and just live in this scenario. What do you know? Who will you be in this scenario? And that's who you are, drawing from all you were."

I realize she has opened up to me, and I'm both honored and uncomfortable with the sincerity. I don't know how this is supposed to help me. I clear my throat. "Well, thank you. Very deep." I blink a few times. "But uhh... RaeChaeline or Clementine? What do you know about that?"

Phoebe shrugs. "They're neither the best nor the worst, like most any human. Most fall in the middle."

"So cryptic."

Phoebe laughs and stands. "I practice the fortune teller thing too much. It's become part of me, I suppose."

I stand. "Thank you. I think."

Phoebe shrugs. "Us forgetful people gotta remember to stick together."

I laugh and wave and leave. Then I realize I still don't know who I'm siding with or what I'm doing. And I'm a little thankful that Phoebe maybe won't remember what we talked about to spill to someone else. I'd like to hope I can trust her, but can never be safe here.

Phoebe closed the door and rested her head against the frame.

It wasn't easy knowing she was about to lose a memory. It was never easy. She looked at her hands; they trembled with what they knew. She was in the middle of some sort of coup and what she remembered was death, so much death. And she couldn't even be sure if it was past death or future death. She couldn't be sure she could trust this boy to save them. She could rush to find a pen and paper, jot down something. But that wasn't her way. Her way was trusting that somehow she still knew, even if she didn't remember. She had to believe that. It'd gotten her here, which, who knows...was maybe something.

Like basic math or her preference for coffee over tea. Like how she was naturally drawn back to her circus wagon each night. She didn't have to remember where she lived, she just felt it.

But it still terrified her knowing she'd lose the memory. It slipped away softly, discreetly, while she rested her head on the door frame. She looked down at her hands. They were shaking, and she didn't know why. She went and sat down. There were two coffee mugs, presumably one hers. She picked one up and took a sip. It was nearly empty. She poured herself another cup.

 DECIDE TO TRY IT. Stop trying to plan out every scenario, and just plan for this one. And in this scenario, I think the first thing I want to do is be with RaeCh.

Not necessarily take her side—I haven't planned that far yet (and if Phoebe's right, planning isn't my thing and doesn't need to be.) But what we have is, well, something. RaeCh had been there for me, kinda, and now I want to be there for her, kinda.

So I head back home.

"Where you been?" RaeCh sounds oddly suspicious, but then again when is she not.

"Took a walk," I partially lie. I guess in this scenario Jasper/Max/me is okay with a little fib.

"You didn't bring home a bird, did you?"

I shake my head. "Not this time."

"Never again," she warns.

I nod. "Right."

"I've been thinking..." she begins, and I wonder if this is another one of her scripted pauses.

"Of course you have."

"...if we're going to kill off a certain...sidekick creature..."

"You're not talking about me, right?"

RaeChaeline shrugs and cracks a half-smile. "I'm being cryptic here."

"Right."

"Well, we're going to need to understand it more. And we just have..." She mutters under her breath something I can't hear. "...days to do so."

"What was that?" I ask.

"A number of days is all I'm saying."

"We already turned in the notes. How long does that mean we have?"

RaeChaeline shrugs. "That's what I'm saying. A number."

"Exactly." I eye her, and for once she dodges my gaze. Is that a hint of uncertainty?

Before I can be sure, she clears her throat, lifts her chin and meets my gaze. "So you need to buddy up with Clementine."

I shake my head, not necessarily in disagreement, just bafflement. "Huh?"

"You're much better with that doting thing than I am."

"You can't act?"

RaeCh makes a gagging noise. "Not with her."

I wonder in this scenario what I'd do. And I make a choice. "I guess I could try..."

"Just remember, it's an act," she says. "No doting for real."

I can't make any promises with that. I don't know what I'd do in that scenario, because I'm not in it yet. But I nod.

"Now you'll want to pay attention to any vulnerabilities they have..." and she continues explaining her plan.

I smile. RaeChaeline is coming back, and maybe I am, too.

# 50

OMETHING I FORGOT: I'm no good with spiders. I remember when it's not Clementine who answers the door, but Claude.

I hear a click after I knock, then the spider scurries up and around the door handle, seeming to beckon me to turn it. So I do, and he leads me down the hall.

I consider smashing one, ya know, for the research RaeCh assigned to me. But I'm not sure what happens to the others then. Do they all turn and attack? Do they all die? Does Clementine die? I'm not quite clear on what sort of symbiotic relationship they may or may not have, and I decide I should probably have more intel before entering the experimental phase of this harebrained scheme.

Clementine and Claude have taken up residence in Dr. Evil's gargantuan home, graduating from the research facility to the main wing. Clementine is splayed out on a decadent couch, munching on a bowl of chocolates. "Do we call you Max or Jasper?"

"Err, does Claude call me...?"

"Don't be rude."

"I mean, Max please."

Clementine smiles. "What brings you here?"

"Came to see how I can help with the grand plan."

"Ahh." Clementine sits up. "She doesn't trust me."

"Huh?"

"Don't worry," Clementine says. "I wouldn't either."

"Oh. Good...?"

Clementine waves her hand at a seat. "Get comfortable. We have company."

I sit at the edge of the chair. I'm not sure I can get comfortable with Claude around.

Dr. Evil walks in and sniffs in distaste. "Oh. You're here."

I don't think he means me.

Clementine smiles. "We were just discussing the horrendous fire on the property. Truly a shame to lose all your research to such an accident."

"Yes, yes." Dr. Evil pats his hair. "Such a shame. May Gep rest in peace and all that."

Clementine looks meaningfully at me. I tense even more. What could she want from me?

"Anyhow, I'll be out for a spell," Dr. Evil continues. "Do clean up after the vermin now."

Clementine lifts her hand and flutters her fingers in a goodbye wave. Once he's gone, she turns to me. "He's pretending. Feigning indifference. No heart whatsoever, wouldn't you say?"

I swallow. "I guess..."

"Anyhow, I'm getting bored. You were so fashionably late, I'm positively antsy. Let's get outta here."

"Where are we going?"

Clementine raises her eyebrows. "You'll see."

We are at the train station. Claude hangs back at a distance. He doesn't like crowds, Clementine says, which I make mental note of in case I want to tell RaeChaeline. Intel.

"See that there?" Clementine points at the train coming in. "That is my ticket out of here."

"What about Claude?"

"Him too."

"I thought he doesn't like crowds."

"Oh no, he could never be in a crowd," Clementine says, oblivious to the issue.

"So you want to get out of town?" I ask.

"I want to see everything," Clementine says. "I've seen one room for years. A lovely room, Claude says, but how many other rooms are there to explore? How many other worlds am I missing?"

"So that's your...toybox?" I try to use her language. "The world?"

"I'm not sure I have a toybox," she says. "Maybe one day I'll find it. Others had years to discover theirs. I just heard stories from Claude and tried to shape them into a toybox. And now, I want all the toyboxes. Then maybe I can pick just one."

I nod. "This a revenge thing, then? Get back at Dr. Evil for locking you up?"

"Oh, he wasn't locking me up," Clementine says. "He was locking up Claude. Or, trying to. If he kept me locked away, Claude would never go far, he figured. He meant well. Just didn't understand Claude."

"Does anyone?"

Clementine shrugs. "He's a mystery. Just like you, like me..." She touches my arm. "...but you know you got wrapped up in something you were never part of?"

"What do you mean?"

"I mean you're not one of us. You're just crafted by one of us."

"A puppet, you mean?"

Clementine smirks. "Perhaps, if an unintentional one."

I remember Jasper's notes. "I called it 'looking with full blinders into the blazing sun.'"

"You're a poet." She smiles, as if delighted to stumble into the presence of one of "the greats" on one of her first outings, only it's just me.

"Too dramatic for that," I correct.

"Still... You understand where we come from. You became bonded against your will, and here you are. Just like the rest of us. So you're different, but you're no different."

"What's that gotta do with anything?"

She doesn't answer the question. "What's your toybox?"

The question I'd been wondering a long time. Jasper had told Max he could build his life elsewhere, far, far away. That "the prophecy is behind us" and the rest of my life is mine for the taking. No fate. No magic. No puppeteering, if we're using Clementine's metaphor.

"I'm supposed to leave all this behind," I say. "Like you and Claude, I guess. But I'm still not sure if that's what I want or if that's what some past version of me wanted."

"Ahh," Clementine says. "The toybox changes over time."

I nod and put my hands in my pockets.

"Do me a favor," Clementine says. "When you find your toybox, tell me what it is. You have my interest piqued."

I fiddle with the radio in my pocket. What would Ferg say? But it isn't supposed to matter anymore. What Ferg wants or RaeCh or Clementine or even Jasper. I need to understand Max, and that is the biggest mystery of all.

# 51

LEMENTINE SENDS ME HOME to "report back." She's not falling for anything, which makes me wonder if what we discussed was real or a show she put on. I can't just believe her. But there has to be some test. Some way to know without tipping our hand that it's a test.

Then I remember RaeChaeline did that before. Never mind that Clementine passed with flying colors that time. The tables have since turned, and we need a new test. But I can borrow from RaeCh's playbook.

"Fancy," I yell when I arrive home. "We're going to Psych Institute!"

I wonder if it's like exposure therapy or something, coming and going without incidence not once, but twice, of my own accord. At least, I hope that's what it is, my heart pounding as we enter again.

She gets us in with her usual charm or persuasion or whatever she uses.

"What'd you find out?" she asks.

"Claude doesn't like crowds...?"

"Neither do I," she says. "What's that gotta do with anything?"

I shrug. "Maybe nothing. Supposedly they wanna get outta town."

"On the run?"

"More like explore." I realize I don't know how to explain it. Whatever Clementine was telling me. "But that wasn't why I brought you here."

RaeChaeline sighs. "Then why are you wasting my time? Get to the point."

"The point is they're onto us," I explain. "They know I was sent by you, so I can't really believe anything they tell me."

"Oh, they passed the first test!" She claps her hands in delight.

I just stand there dumbfounded, watching her all giddy; finally I sputter a word: "What?"

RaeChaeline nods. "Our competition is clever. We'll just have to be even more so. Well, I will. You keep being you."

I fold my arms across my chest. "One of these days you gotta let me in on your schemes."

"I work alone..." she claims.

"You clearly don't."

RaeChaeline plops down and sighs. "What'd ya bring me here for? I'm getting tired."

"Well, I was thinking we need a test."

"Obviously," she says.

"Obviously. Right." I crouch to a squat in front of her, not quite ready to get comfortable in this place. "Something that shows her true motives and if she can be trusted."

RaeChaeline frowns. "She can't be trusted. She killed Gep."

I cringe. Right. That last part was my own anti-RaeCh plan. Oops.

"But her motives, that's a good one. What would she do with all our naive friends following her?"

"What would you do?" I ask.

RaeCh blinks, not tracking what that's gotta do with anything. "I had them," she clarifies. "And I was gonna save Gep and all of us. Now...now I don't want them. I don't want...anything."

It occurs to me what could be a test for Clementine. A dangerous one, though; it could upend everything. "RaeCh...just how do you get in here?"

RaeChaeline pats her hair and sits straighter. "I have information Dr. Wise would find valuable. I dole out a little here and there, a short-term rental, as-needed sorta thing."

"This place gives me the chills," I say.

"Oh, I know; that's just a bonus." She laughs.

I give a fake laugh. "But how do you feel here? Safe? Comfortable?"

She glares at me. "I don't belong here if that's what you're insinuating."

"Not what I meant!"

"I'm grieving the loss of a friend, not delusional."

I'm not sure those are mutually exclusive, but that's beside the point. "I mean, as a test. Say you get locked up. We see what Clementine does with that info. She thinks you're trapped and she has all of us at her whims. And she has to prove if she really wants us all in our own 'toybox' or whatever, or if she's okay with collateral."

RaeChaeline purses her lips. "Hmm. There's an idea. When she leaves me here to rot all the others see her for who she is. Scoundrel." She purses her lips. "How good are you at lying?"

"That's the biggest problem with the plan."

"That's what I like about you," she says. Hooray, a compliment?

"Always know exactly where you stand..." She pauses, considering, then jumps up and pats my shoulder. "Well, guess that plan won't work."

That should have been my clue she was acting.

"We'll keep thinking, though. We'll come up with something."

She opens the door, and I follow. Only, she stops. She pulls out the key, studies it, and smiles. Then she looks at me with a laugh and tosses it into the hall. She slams the door shut on both of us.

"What are you—" I push past her and hit the door, which is of course locked.

"That should do the trick." She gives me an accomplished smile. "Can't botch this up if you're stuck in here with me."

# 52

**HY WOULD YOU DO THAT?**" I ask.

RaeChaeline shrugs. "Why not? It's a test."

"If neither of us are out, how will she know to consider rescuing us or leaving us to rot? How will *we* know what she decides or when?"

RaeChaeline squints. "Hmm. Not sure."

"*Not sure?* You never do a plan when you're *not sure*. You always have a dozen steps thought through plus a dozen backup plans."

"Well, the backup plan is I can coax the staff to let us out at any time. Obviously we're not really trapped. Just...putting ourselves in time out for a spell."

My breathing becomes a staccato, hitting me with all the reasons I cannot trust this Fancy, just like the last one. Why I shouldn't have willingly walked into this place ever again. No escape. Brightness. Darkness. It's all hitting me again, and I just want out.

"Sit down," she says. "You're making me nervous."

I don't know what to do. So, I sit. I wipe my sweaty hands on my pants.

"Inhale..." she says.

I do.

"...exhale..."

I do.

"Anyhow, I don't have a dozen steps," she clarifies. "I don't have a backup plan for everything. Never have."

"Not possible," I choke out.

"Just, maybe five steps and one or two backup plans."

"No, you always know what to do. You always pivot perfectly."

"It's an act," she says. "Sure, I want control, and I want to have a dozen plans, don't get me wrong. But not even I can pull that off. But when perception is everything, I gotta pretend. All. The. Time. I can't let up for a moment."

I gulp, trying to pull out of my own thoughts to listen to hers instead. But I keep getting stuck in the loop of tying them to something that can get me out of here. "That sounds painful," I manage.

"I gotta responsibly handle this...whatever it is I've been given. I messed up once, and I can't again. It costs too much." RaeChaeline nods. "Painful, I suppose, yes. My cross to bear. So, don't tell anyone this, and more importantly don't give up your faith in my supposedly-dozen-step, dozen-plans mmkay? I need you to keep believing in me."

She places a hand on my shoulder, which is almost reassuring. I manage a glance at her. "I think I believe your act more than whatever you just told me, so no worries."

RaeChaeline smiles. "Right where I want you."

"Well, yeah, you locked me in here; what do you expect?" I try a laugh. It doesn't feel right. "Get comfortable. You're stuck with me."

*RaeChaeline brought Gep around, a bit at least. She didn't encourage him to take solace in reaching out to the other woman—it was too late for a chance at that. RaeChaeline didn't encourage him to meet his son. Viel had taken the woman and son as his own; true to Viel's words, the woman had gone toward something more reliable—generational wealth—instead of something as frivolous as love.*

*Instead, RaeChaeline encouraged Gep that they could figure out this together, that they could best Dr. Viel and use their words toward his ruin one day.*

*"You're not alone in this, Gep," she soothed. She rested her hand on his shoulder. "Just hold yourself together. Put on a façade until it's reality. It's all about perception. That's all the world sees of us, of anyone, really."*

*He brushed her hand off. "Easy for you to say."*

*But in time, he had no choice but to believe her words. He had to hope again. Obsession, desperation, something along those lines.*

*Eventually, they were feverishly studying again the ways that they'd changed Gep. The strings they'd unraveled.*

*They didn't notice that RaeCh had stopped aging. Of course they couldn't, that takes time. They didn't notice that the way people saw her had changed; or rather, it stayed the same while she changed.*

*It took time to realize that the words she'd offered a friend had entangled themselves into her being. That perception was everything to her now, quite literally impacting the way people saw her; hence, her reputation must precede her to make her invulnerable.*

*For now, though, she was just a friend, sitting with Gep as he despaired and trying to offer him a glimpse of hope, a glimpse of camaraderie that she didn't realize would cost so much.*

# 53

E WAIT A LONG TIME. When you're in a windowless room, you can't really be sure how long it is. Just, too long.

An orderly finally notices and brings us food. Twice. I'm not really sure what their schedule is for it. Has it been half a day? A whole day? Two?

By the second time, RaeChaeline realizes we could be stuck a long time if we wait for Clementine to discover our absence and piece together our whereabouts.

"Tell Dr. Wise that RaeChaeline needs to talk."

The orderly stiffens. "Dr. Wise is otherwise occupied."

"When he has a moment."

"Dr. Wise sees his patients on his schedule."

Pfft. RaeChaeline looks miffed. "I'm no patient. I'm intel. And if he wants it…"

Dr. Wise approaches the door and waves off the orderly. "…if I want it, I know where to find you now, don't I? You returned the key, RaeChaeline. What possible leverage do you have, now that I have you?"

And that's when I realize we are truly trapped.

RaeChaeline realizes it, too. She bangs on the door as Dr. Wise leaves. "I just need you to tell my enemy I'm stuck here!" she yells. But whether someone hears or not doesn't matter.

She slumps in front of the door and lifts her gaze to meet mine. "What are you looking at?"

"We're really stuck here?" I ask. "Not just fake stuck here?"

"You heard him."

"But that's, like, something you planned, right? To trick me into thinking we're stuck. Not because we're really...stuck."

RaeChaeline raises an eyebrow. "Your faith in my foresight is truly unrivaled."

I cross my arms, holding myself together. Willing myself to not become the darkness, which is silly because of course I can't. Nick isn't here. But all I feel is this need to hold myself together.

# 54

LEMENTINE WAS GETTING BORED. Or rather, Claude was getting bored. They were free now. Why wait? Why sit in this mansion, mere yards from their former prison, when they could explore the world?

And so, Clementine was bored.

For years, Claude had been her connection with the outside world, her calm reassurance that one day they would be free. Now that they were, Claude wasn't her calm reassurance. He was an anxious energy pulsing through her veins, begging to get out of this place.

Or, maybe it was just her. Maybe she had been calm with Claude, and now that she was free she was antsy and it fed into Claude. Sometimes she couldn't be sure where one of them stopped and the other began.

So Clementine and Claude got out of the house and went, where else? To the circus. Claude mostly stayed in the field, though some spiders clung to Clementine for the show. She watched Analiese, ringmaster, live her life, so comfortable in her own skin. So certain of what she was there for. She watched Nick stumble through his routine...oh, quite confident in what he was doing, just not quite so confident as to why. He was here because it was a place, and because Analiese was there, and Julia was sometimes there. And Julia was here because Analiese and Nick were there.

Belonging, it's called. When you're more than a puppet to someone. Like Claude was to Clementine, or like Clementine was to Claude. That's what they had here.

Julia was not new to the feeling, though she'd been looking a long time. Phoebe so assuredly had it within herself, and she didn't even have a Claude. RaeChaeline used to have it, until Clementine made the mishap permanent. Max wanted it more than anything. And Sylas was oblivious to the concept.

They all circled it in their own way. And Clementine watched through Claude from the outside. And she wanted it. Claude wasn't enough. Or Clementine wasn't enough for Claude. She wasn't sure.

They needed more.

# 55

RAECHAELINE HAD GONE TO SLEEP. I imagined it'd be a fitful one with all that's happened, all the turmoil around and in her lately. But she sleeps deeply instead. The picture of calm, like an infant who had used up all its energy in a fit right before. An infant who would surely wake with energy anew.

With RaeCh sleeping soundly, that leaves me to stay awake, to fret, worry, pace. And I do. I do for so long, at least I assume so, until I'm worn out. Yet she still sleeps. I'm pretty sure it'd be more effective if she would fret while I slept, but I attempt to pull my own weight around here.

Eventually I tire of pacing, and I sit.

I don't even notice myself drifting off, with nothing to show for it when RaeCh awakes.

I wake what seems like mere minutes later. I'm being prodded, but when I open my eyes it's not RaeCh. I'm being strapped to something by staff. A wheelchair. I swivel my head to the side and see RaeCh is in a wheelchair as well, though she sleeps on.

They must have known we'd both fallen asleep. They must have been waiting. They wheel me out of the room. I should have stayed awake.

I'm still groggy, which I worry means they gave me something. Shouldn't I be wide awake in a situation like this, from the nerves? Shouldn't RaeCh wake up kicking and screaming, getting us out of this mess?

But I wasn't, and she hadn't.

The man in charge walks into the room: Dr. Wise. Someone hovers behind him, too.

I blink and try to look around, but my head and eyes won't cooperate.

"So this is who we captured in the trap," Dr. Wise explains.

"Him?" the other man says.

I wonder if this will be like the torture chamber RaeCh had me in once. I glance around, and don't see any scalpels, but then again there are plenty of cabinets and drawers they could be in.

But the man says, "He's nothing."

I breathe a sigh of relief, for once grateful to be dismissed, deemed so insignificant.

"But he could be something, yes?" Dr. Wise says. "He knows more than he should. He has no connections..."

I take offense to that part. I'd like to hope someone would care—Ferg, Analiese, RaeCh, even Clementine.

"...he's the perfect guinea pig."

I don't like the sound of that, but the figure with Dr. Wise is more agreeable. "Hmm. You may have a point."

Dr. Wise nods, and turns a surgical light to shine in my eyes. I blink and struggle. I can't get loose, but I'm not using reason at the time. I get lucky, though, because then I feel my pocket. And I remember.

"What makes him so different from Clementine, though?" The man who lurks behind finally leans in. Dr. Evil.

"We know more now than we did then."

Dr. Evil nods. "True, true."

A nurse approaches with a needle, pricks me. She takes a vial of blood and leaves. The doctors leave behind her, still conversing about the "possibilities" I introduce. I cling to the hope in my pocket, presuming I get a chance for this knowledge to be useful.

I drift off again.

# 56

WAKE BACK IN THE ROOM we started in. I'm still strapped to the chair and take a moment to assess. My waist, shins, and elbows are tied to the chair, designed to prevent more macro movements like escape; but if the right person got just close enough, I could maybe dole out a decent kick or grab a key or weapon or something of use. I add that to my list of information I hope will come in handy soon, which reminds me... My pocket.

I struggle to reach, but my arm doesn't twist like that.

I look around. "RaeCh!"

"Shh." She gestures with her head toward the ceiling, and I look. Ahh. Cameras. That's how they knew we were asleep.

She stretches her arms against the restraints towards the wheels and hobbles my way with grunts and jostles. Finally she settles next to me, her chair the opposite direction so we're staring face to face, inches apart.

I change to a whisper. "Did they hurt you? Are you okay?"

"Simple blood draw," she says. "Research, probably. You?"

"Same."

RaeChaeline's brows furrow. "But you're..." She shakes her head. "Must be to contrast or something. Odd."

I notice her tense, though. She knows something she's not telling me. As always.

Which reminds me, I have something to tell her. "Is it safe to talk, you think?"

"Quietly. If they have audio we don't want them to hear."

I nod. "I know how to get help."

She smiles dryly. "Would have been nice to know before we were tied up, but I'll take it."

"Can you reach in my pocket?"

She wheels around behind me and reaches her hand through the back. I wriggle up a bit to help. It's tight. She can just touch it. "What is it?"

"The radio to Ferg," I answer.

"I'm not even gonna ask why you're carrying that around when you refuse to talk to him."

"A thank you would be nice."

She squints in thought, then nods. "Once we're out of here, I'll consider it."

That didn't change the problem that we couldn't reach it, though. I slump back down into my seat.

"Wait. Try again," she says.

I don't see the point until she tells me...

"Maybe I can reach the radio buttons. We gotta try."

"Oh, yeah," I say dryly. "Just so they don't notice on camera we're doing anything weird."

I sit back up, and she reaches again. More determined or at least more focused than before. She feels around, and thankfully she finds it.

"Say something," she hisses.

"You say something," I counter.

"He doesn't care about me." She pushes the button again.

And I suppose she's right. "Ferg, can you hear me?" I whisper.

She releases the button. Nothing.

We try again. Still nothing.

RaeCh slumps her head onto my wheelchair handles.

"It was worth a shot," I say forlornly.

RaeCh shakes her head. "You have to be louder, I think."

"They'll hear, too, then."

"...maybe." She taps her fingers, scheming again.

I remember what Phoebe said, about hanging with planners too much, and I wonder. Whatever I say could bring rescue or could alert our captors to our only hope of rescue. My words have to be good. Like, RaeCh-plan good. And yet...

"Push the button," I whisper.

"Huh?" RaeCh asks.

"I'll try one more time." It's the truth, kinda. She probably assumes I mean a whisper and thinks nothing of it. She presses the button.

"RaeCh, uhmm..." I say, loudly this time. "...It's Max, remember."

RaeCh's lifts her head, perks up. She doesn't like it, but she doesn't release the button, either.

"Listen..." I keep going, winging it. "You and I, we gotta escape Psych Institute, but it's really hopeless. No one knows we're here, no one knows we're trapped. I need you to keep your wits about you and figure something out. Okay?"

RaeCh's eyes are wide, her nose is flaring, but she hasn't stopped me yet. She probably hasn't finished planning to stop me yet.

I need to know he heard. I need to know. So I add, "Just, no need to be all showy about it, but just whisper to me, okay? Tell me you're in. Just a whisper."

RaeCh realizes that's her cue. She lifts her finger from the button and sighs. "Okayyy".

Better yet, I hear a clicking noise from the radio, and then a soft and muffled "okay." A pause. Then: "Hang in there."

I smile at RaeCh, and more importantly, she's smiling back at me. He heard. We have a chance, if my words didn't mess this up.

My mind goes into overdrive worrying about how he could possibly get us out of here, how he could get any help when people won't remember anything he tells them, or how we'll last until help of whatever variety arrives.

But it's something I can't do anything about. I just have to wait uncomfortably in this chair and hold out hope that I'll survive until someone else figures it out.

I try to rest a little easier knowing that I figured out this one domino on my own; I just need to wait for the rest to follow.

57

ESIDES MAX AND RAECHAELINE, there was only one person who would remember him after his death. He shuddered: Clementine.

So Ferg wrote a note and delivered it to the nearest spider. He watched and wondered if it was the *right* spider, or just some random spider. It stuck around, climbing on and off the note, never moving far.

Ten minutes later he noticed two other spiders arriving. Another five minutes, and there were three more. (One was so tiny it could hardly be of any assistance, but that didn't seem to matter.) They collectively clambered with the thing and began to move. Ferg only hoped it was quick enough.

Meanwhile, word reached Clementine before the note did. *Ferg needs you. Ferg is trying to get a message to you.*

Clementine perked up. She was bored (or Claude was bored), so she wasn't going to wait hours for the note to arrive. She raced out the door and to the convenience store where she'd first seen the radio. And she just so happened to bump into none other than Ferg there. He smiled, then frowned, realizing the predicament.

She purchased a new radio, and once it was in a bag with a receipt, he left while she waited for him to get a distance away.

Then, wondering what the plan was and how they would get in touch, she found the spiders who were hauling the note. She picked it up and read where to meet him, went to the tree, and saw him off a distance, under another tree. He waved. She waved.

Had something changed? Did he remember?

She picked up the radio. "I thought Max was our go-between now," she said.

"Max has run into some trouble," he said.

Clementine's face paled, and Claude perked up, too. Where had they last seen Max? Why hadn't she worried more when he hadn't been seen? She should be more paranoid, *we should be more paranoid*, she told Claude. He agreed.

"Him and RaeChae are trapped at Psych Institute. How do we get them out?"

*How do we, how do we?* Claude's eyes lit up at the challenge, at the adventure of it all. Clementine patted the closest one on the head in reassurance. "We'll find a way. But we need the others, too."

Claude let out a sigh. *With others isn't as fun.*

Clementine nodded. Shrugged. This wasn't the message she had hoped for from Ferg. She'd wanted something...more...

And somehow, in that moment, Ferg read her mind or Claude betrayed her secrets to him, and Ferg interrupted her thoughts.

"I try not to remember before."

"We don't have to rehash this conversation," she said. *Shut up, Claude,* she told him for good measure, though Claude maintained his innocence.

"It was a terrible childhood no one should relive," Ferg added.

Clementine bit her lip.

"Which is why I try to forget the little girl I found before I left."

Clementine's face grew hot. *No. He doesn't remember.*

"With the wildest curls and her spider friends," he continued.

She swiped at her eyes and picked up the radio. "What an odd coincidence."

She looked across the way at him, and he nodded. "Quite."

"The way Claude tells it you were thrown out."

"Maybe," he said. "Like I said, I try to forget."

"It's not worth remembering," she agreed.

He nodded.

Clementine sniffled. Cleared her throat. "Anyhow, enough of this drama. We've got a rescue to plan."

"Sure. Right." He looked down where Claude was climbing onto his shoes. Then he added, "But...You're worth remembering, though. Don't forget that."

*They still didn't understand it; of course they didn't. Nothing was revealing itself, nothing was adding up. They may catch a pattern here or there, but as soon as they did, it would be disproven or twisted into a shape they never intended. (Why do you think RaeCh was so careful in resurrecting Gep? She's learned.)*

*The magic kept working under the surface, leading us to the point of Gep on a slab at Dr. Evil's while the magic eats away at RaeChaeline.*

*But first, it led to Gep approaching Viel's house in desperation, banging at the door.*

*"Viel. Viel! You have to help us."*

*A spider crawled through the doorway, and Gep scowled at it. But it was closely followed by Gep's intended audience.*

*"Hush!" Dr. Viel yelled as he opened the door. "Have you no decorum? I've lost my wife and my daughter in one night. My son lost..."*

*Gep interrupted under his breath. "...my son..."*

*"My son," Viel iterated again. "He lost his mother.*

*Have you no compassion?" Viel looked down at the spider on the threshold, frowned, and stepped on it.*

*"It's got ahold of RaeCh, too," Gep said. "Viel, the curse is spreading..."*

*Viel laughed, but this time it was a haunting, sad laugh. "The curse. It takes too many, creates too many freaks of nature. It's more hungry than you or I."*

*"You have to help us stop it."*

*Viel sighed. "The only research I'd be doing is to stamp this evil out by any means necessary. Lock it up if I must! Until the power can be understood, it cannot be controlled."*

*"At whose expense?"*

*"Yours, apparently. RaeChaeline's." Viel shrugged. "We all have our burdens to bear. I'm not totally heartless; it's cost me, too."*

*Two more spiders scurry across the doorway and out of reach. Dr. Evil scowls at them.*

*Gep shook. "I'll figure it out. RaeCh will figure it out, you know she's unstoppable. We'll figure it out before you can catch hold of it."*

*Viel shook his head. "You'll... You really think..." Then he got hard, cold. "You will never amount to anything, Gep."*

*Viel started to shut the door, then paused, shook his finger. "Unless, maybe... This is too good... Maybe if you start a circus. A freak show." Viel winked. "But, even that's a longshot."*

# 58

HIS TIME I'M AWAKE. Wide awake. Whatever concoction they'd put in our system was long gone, so when they wheel us away we get front row seats to where they are taking us in the building. Maybe that's of no use, but I tell myself every piece of intel could be critical in an escape, so I pay attention.

Down the hall, to the right, and a short left.

This time, we're in the room together.

"You got lucky!" Dr. Wise says.

Somehow I don't feel so lucky.

"Your blood is a match."

Now I really don't feel so lucky. "Please," I say.

Dr. Evil enters the room with another orderly, and RaeCh perks up. I wonder if she knew he was here before now.

"Manners get you nothing around here," Dr. Evil says.

The nurse approaches RaeCh and begins to set something up with a needle injected into her arm, and I see where this is heading.

"Don't do this," RaeChaeline pleads. "Each time we've tried, it's been worse than before. You know it."

249

"Like a lightbulb, though," Dr. Evil says. "Who knows if today we see a spark."

"I'm not very bright," I try. It doesn't get a laugh.

The nurse approaches me and pricks my arm. The blood begins to flow, from RaeCh to me.

"Others dream of this opportunity," Dr. Wise reassures.

"Others would kill for this opportunity," Dr. Evil amends.

"You can't even begin to understand what I'll kill for," RaeChaeline threatens, to no avail. It would've scared me in their shoes, but being in mine, it almost makes me feel invincible. Almost.

"One day you'll understand," Dr. Evil says. "In fact, there was one day you did understand I dare say, RaeChaeline."

They all leave the room.

"What did happen, those other failed lightbulb times?" I ask RaeCh.

RaeCh shrugs. "Gep...me...all of us. All of this."

"So, I'll become one of you?"

"None of the other times were a success, understand. All of them twisted, transformed into something we never planned. That's why we're like this." She sighs. "You'll become something. But we can't say for sure what."

I grasp at a straw. "You gotta try, RaeCh. Your words do things."

"My words are a weapon as bad as this science experiment."

"I trust your words more than this. Please...for me."

RaeCh closes her eyes. Her brow furrows. She clenches her fists. She decides to try, to risk it: "Help is coming for us," she says. "My blood has no effect."

Then she opens her eyes and stares at the ceiling. "They're here."

I look up too and see it. A spider, watching.

# 59

THE PLAN WAS MANY: essentially throw every option out there and see what sticks.

They would try inconspicuous, they would try force, and every option in between.

Clementine via Claude: the surveillance.

Ferg, Analiese, and Nick: the rescue squad.

Sylas and Sullivan: the distraction.

Julia and Phoebe: operation lights out.

Each person wrote notes to themselves of the objective ("Rescue RaeChae and Max") and their own particular part in it. That way, if they got separated and forgot, they had something to go on.

Claude scoped out the facilities ahead of time, and Clementine drew a map to where they were keeping Max and RaeChae. Their orders were to try to reach them without force, simply by being quicker than the competition so that they'd forget. If that failed, Analiese was there to buy them a bit more time. And if that didn't work, Julia and Phoebe would hopefully help Nick get further in, though that would really be a flip of a coin and they'd have to be ready to pivot and use the chaos of the moment to their advantage.

They were as ready as they'd ever be. The lofty goal was that every last one of them gets out.

It started with Sullivan. He approached the front desk with Sylas, who nodded at a particular receptionist over another. That was the signal that this one had the eyes of a hawk, and they'd want to distract her the most.

The receptionists glanced up. The men approaching weren't of much interest. One asked for directions, and they began to fill him in.

He didn't need to affect anything, really, except the window in which they noticed the intruders' presence. As long as the Forgettable got close enough before they realized, they wouldn't even remember later.

As they got into the monotonous droning of "is it west or north, or perhaps northwest? No, it must be northeast," the rescue squad rushed past. And of course they saw. They yelled "stop" for a moment and nearly ran after them, but then the memory faded to black and they wondered why they were on alert with a couple guys simply asking how to get to the diner a few blocks away. The receptionists returned their attention to them, and it's kind of a "northwesterly eastern direction, I suppose." The man thanked them and left with his friend. The receptionists rolled their eyes and moved on with their day. Nothing to see here.

Meanwhile, Sullivan was beaming. He'd done it. He'd gotten the directions, kinda, and that was important to rescue Max and RaeChaeline. After saving people not once, but twice now, he was on his way to becoming a proper hero.

Clementine offered a high five, and then she froze. "Oh, no," she said, and Sullivan wondered what he did wrong.

"I'm sorry?" he offered.

"They've been moved," Clementine said. "They're heading the wrong way."

Sullivan breathed a sigh of relief that he didn't mess anything up. But that didn't matter if the plan is messed up, anyhow.

"I gotta go in," Clementine said.

"But the Forgettable isn't here," Sullivan said. "The directions won't work without him."

"They'll have to."

"They'll remember you're breaking in," Sylas added. "It'll put the whole building on high alert and render the Forgettable pointless."

"By subtlety or by force, remember. We're getting through."

# 60

ULLIVAN DID HIS LINE AGAIN; he forgot the directions already, he claimed. Not that it made any difference this time.

When Clementine and Sylas rushed past, the receptionists rushed after, leaving Sullivan in the entryway alone. Or, almost alone. Claude was beginning his entry as well. He descended from the ceiling and entered through the doorway and crawled out of nooks and crannies no one paid any attention to. And he followed Clementine. Sullivan waved at him and exited the building.

Meanwhile, Clementine and Sylas were running down a hall here, taking a turn there. Orderlies began to give chase. There was no denying as they raced past that they wouldn't be getting out the way they came.

Analiese, the Forgettable, and Nick were nearly to their destination just a few doors away when they noticed the commotion. A security officer rushed past them toward, well, someone else...?

That's when they realized something wasn't right.

"You take Nick, see what the trouble is," Analiese told Ferg. "Help however you can. I can fend for myself and get the others."

So Ferg and Nick went back the way they came, and Analiese carried on. She heard the chaos behind her and considered turning back. But the note was clear, and she stood in front of a door now that must be the one from the map.

She yelled in. "RaeChae? Max?"

Nothing.

She turned the knob, but it was locked, and she was fairly certain the key was too far away.

She pounded on the door. "It's Analiese. Can you hear me?"

Still nothing.

She crept down the hall to an empty office, and crouched. She heard someone run past. Just in time.

She remembered another locked door once, Max's old apartment. She couldn't blow her cover then for him. Couldn't possibly pick the lock. But now...

Analiese lifted her index finger, looked at the doorknob nearby and compared it to the one she'd seen earlier. She squeezed her index finger, molded it like clay until it stretched far past the fingernail into a very thin line. Almost as if it were a key.

She listened. No one coming. Whatever was causing a ruckus, it was far enough away.

She crept back to the door and slid her finger into the lock. Oh, it was the wrong shape of course. It wasn't the key to this particular room. But it was something much better—a skeleton key of sorts. She slowly nudged the tumbler and pins just so.

It takes patience and precision, but that's what Analiese had been training in her whole life. She worked her magic until the inner mechanisms were a shape that would turn. And then, she opened the door.

Empty. They weren't here.

She should have known, what with the commotion elsewhere.

She needed to get to the action right away.

Then, the lights went out.

# 61

LEMENTINE AND THAT QUIRKY SYLAS GUY that hangs around pop into our room, and I don't think I've ever been so thankful to see those two. But it wouldn't be that easy. Plenty of staff follow them.

"Help!" I try, as if there's any point.

Clementine rushes over and begins pulling needles out of our arms and loosing us from our ties, as if it makes any difference.

"What did they do to me?" I say.

"I don't know," Clementine says. "I don't know."

"It didn't work," Sylas says. "It doesn't work."

I stand up, so relieved to be out of that chair. RaeCh stands, too, then stumbles a bit. Clementine catches her. "Let's get you out of here."

"How?" RaeChaeline says skeptically. We all look at the security officers in the door, the orderlies and nurses peeking in behind them. We aren't going anywhere any time soon.

And then, we see it. First their ankles, then their knees. That's when some of them notice, too. Claude is taking over.

A shriek. They look around, look down, and nearly in unison begin brushing off all these spiders. Clementine pushes through them, and we follow. At first I am careful to watch my step, though I see somehow Claude avoids our path. He somehow makes a way while getting in their way.

We run into the Forgettable and Nick.

"Stay back," Clementine tells Ferg. "We don't want them to forget this."

Then, the lights go out.

# 62

ICK FELT IT SLIPPING AWAY. Himself, drifting out of his solid state and into an absence, a presence he was too familiar with. He trembled. Julia had done it, and he had to be brave, just a little longer.

Almost as soon as it started, he felt himself solidifying, falling, hitting the floor. He looked up. Hallway of a medical facility. Psych Institute. Emergency lights gleaming. A generator. He stumbled to his feet and turned. There they were. Mere yards away, hundreds of spiders were taking over the hospital staff, and just behind them stood the rest of the team: Clementine, Forgettable, Sylas, RaeChae, Max.

"Run!" Clementine called to him.

Then he realized, if the staff get away from the Forgettable before he does, they won't remember which way that group ran, but they sure would remember which way he went.

He turned and ran down the hall. A body slammed into him, and he fell to the floor. He looked up. Analiese!

She climbed off him. "Sorry! I'll fix that."

He had no idea what she did to him yet. "Later."

"Right."

They both stood up. Two security guards were running toward them. "Not again..." she said.

They ran down the stairway to the getaway cars. Phoebe behind the wheel of one, with Julia and Sullivan in back.

Analiese climbed into the driver's seat of the other car, and Nick got in with the others.

"Where's the rest?" Julia asked.

"Other side," Nick said.

"What door?"

"No idea."

There was a knock on the glass, and they jumped. Analiese.

She opened the door. "You all are sitting ducks. Go. I'll get them."

"We can't lea..." Julia began.

But Analiese wouldn't listen. "Julia, don't let him get trapped here again."

Julia nodded. "Phoebe, drive!"

Phoebe obeyed. Nick began to climb out, but Julia held him back. "Not this time," she said. "You've done enough."

## 63

NALIESE HAD CLIMBED INTO the second getaway car while Nick hopped into the first. They were supposed to wait for the others. Everyone gets out: that was the goal, Clementine said. But right now, Analiese didn't owe everyone. Sure, she hoped everyone got out. But sometimes you have to make tough choices.

One of the lives she owed she could face head-on, consciously. She couldn't let Nick get trapped here again. They had a deal.

The other one she could just kind of glance at in her mind's peripherals: Julia. But she could barely admit it before setting it to the side.

Either way, both of them were there, sitting ducks in that jampacked vehicle. Rendered unnecessary, she could claim if challenged on it later.

She climbed out of her car and rushed to the other, banged on the window.

Julia opened the door. Julia. Something gnawed at Analiese. She owed her, too. But she had to push that back.

"You all are sitting ducks. Go. I'll get them."

Julia opened her mouth to protest. Of course she would. "We can't lea..."

"Julia, don't let him get trapped here again." She knew how to play their weaknesses, their care for someone else, to her own ends. But it was for *good* ends.

Julia nodded. No more argument. "Phoebe, drive!"

Phoebe began to pull away, and Analiese stepped back. She saw Nick trying to climb out and Julia holding him back. They would be safe. For now.

She wondered how many times she would have to owe them before it felt like enough, before the gnawing feeling left. She worried there was no limit.

Analiese turned. Guards now stood between her and the other car.

*Their loss*, she thought. "Hey, boys...take it easy on me, why don't ya."

# 64

LL OF US GET OUT, Clementine thought. *All of us.*

The guards were already disregarding Claude and heading their way. They all ran.

"Stick with Ferg," she yelled. "We can't afford to forget right now."

They rounded a corner and found themselves face to face with Drs. Wise and Evil.

"Such a disappointment," Dr. Evil said. "I expected more of you."

"All of you," Dr. Wise added.

Dr. Evil shrugged.

The guards caught up from behind and surrounded them, still brushing off the spiders.

"We don't belong to you," Clementine said. "You can't just keep us here."

A spider approached Dr. Wise, and he lifted his foot over it.

Dr. Evil grabbed his arm and pulled him back. "Don't crush it."

Dr. Wise glowered at him, then turned back to Clementine. "You don't belong to anyone. That's your greatest weakness."

Max laughed. "You see a mob of people and spiders—spiders, mostly—raiding this place for us, and you think we belong to no one?"

RaeChaeline smiled and whispered in Max's ear.

"Let's see, if I recall correctly..." Dr. Evil pointed at Ferg. "You'll make me forget this moment. Shame, really. I'll have to visit your cell often to bask in it." He pointed at Clementine. "You keep escaping my grasp, but always at the hand of someone else. I can take care of that in one fell swoop here, it appears." Next he pointed at what he assumed was RaeCh. "And you just look like a whipper snapper when you're mostly a bag of bones at this point like myself." Then Dr. Evil smiled. "Anyone else I should care about?"

Dr. Wise cleared his throat. "That guy thinks he sees how things work." The spider climbed his arm. He rolled his eyes and smacked it. It fell to the ground. Where it landed, two spiders crawled away.

Dr. Evil didn't notice. "Best case scenario then, we cut open one of these folks and he can tell us how their brains work, give us a head start on our research. Where's the bad news? Where's the big rescue?"

"You're right," Max jumped in. "It's over. We get it."

Clementine opened her mouth, but Max shook his head.

"What are you going to do to us?" Max said.

The hundreds of spiders approached the group, and Claude saw what no one else did: RaeChaeline sneaking behind the doctors, while they all assumed she was trapped and forlorn like the rest. They only saw what they expected to see.

While Dr. Evil waxed eloquent about finishing the blood transfusion on Max, RaeChaeline wrapped her arm around his throat. He gasped.

"You said it," she said. "You're a bag of bones like me."

"No one has to get hurt," Clementine jumped in. "Just let us all go."

RaeChaeline nodded.

"You don't scare us," Dr. Wise said.

"Let them go!" Dr. Evil interjected.

"What?" Dr. Wise looked skeptical.

"You have no idea what she's capable of." Dr. Evil gave an uneasy smile.

The group walked out from around the guards to stand behind RaeChae.

"Wait..." RaeChaeline said. "Seeing as you're being all reasonable about this..."

"Just let me go," Dr. Evil said.

"Oh, you'll like this." RaeChaeline licked her lips. "I'll let you have one of us. Just one."

Max's stomach clenched. "RaeCh, don't..."

"Take Clementine for whatever research you want. Let the rest of us go, and Clementine stays."

Clementine's eyes widened. "RaeCh..."

"Do it now! Guarantee no one else gets hurt here, Clementine."

The security officers stepped forward, cautiously at first, then more confidently. Ferg and Sylas pushed in front of Clementine.

Max took a step that direction, but paused. What would he do in this scenario? And he doesn't know...

Clementine was frozen. She should run. She should leave.

Everyone gets out. That was the plan. They wouldn't leave her here.

Ferg and Sylas were no match for the security team. And Max stood frozen. And Claude was too slow, still yards away. And RaeChaeline didn't care at all.

It wasn't much of a fight at this point. The officers grabbed Clementine and took her away, holding the others back.

"You can't do this!" she yelled. "Everyone gets out."

"Not quite everyone." RaeChae backed up, still holding onto Dr. Evil by the neck. "Let's go," she told the rest.

They were ready to fight through security again, ready to try and hope.

But Max in his frozen state saw what none of them do. He saw that they'd lost any advantage they had. And they needed to leave with their own lives before they lost them. "RaeCh is right. We gotta go. There's no helping now."

RaeChaeline threw Dr. Evil at Dr. Wise.

WE ALL RUN. Sylas and Ferg pause a moment, stumble, but eventually they run, too. Each and every last one of us run.

We hop into the car that Analiese has waiting and let her drive away.

*It took time. Years. First to identify even a semblance of what was happening. That words about Gep would twist and leave their mark, not just on him but on any in his path.*

*Then to plan, fail, and plan more how to use it to their advantage instead of against them. Then one day, Viel said it himself: a circus.*

*That was their chance at success, the words that RaeCh could twist into prophecy. And she took it.*

*RaeCh worked on a lock-tight contract and tested one after another on herself. It had to be something so certain that the magic couldn't twist its words.*

*Over time she added one restriction after another: "binding," "lifelong," "irrevocable." Until they had hemmed the magic in.*

*Eventually, one contract worked. It ensured that words about Gep expanded, and in the case of those who agreed to these words, Gep's words regarding them could take effect with more or less certainty, too. The magic would finally be bound in their own grasp.*

*Lastly, they just needed others like them, performers. Those suffering, too, perhaps—from the same curse or another—those also looking for a place of freedom and belonging.*

*It was all coming together, one domino at a time.*

# 65

HEN WE SEPARATE FROM FERG, I'm left with this gnawing guilt and the notes I'd scribbled on the drive. That Clementine didn't make it out. Others, I'm sure, are left with less. They may know we're down a person, but they may not realize who to blame. RaeCh may not even feel the satisfaction of her revenge.

It only takes a few hours for Claude to settle in. He creeps into the old Trencher home. First one spider atop the rug, then another in the corner.

At first we worry he's here for some sort of revenge, but he doesn't try anything. He's just here.

Eventually, it's easier to say where Claude isn't than where he is.

He isn't outside of this house. He isn't on me or RaeCh technically, though he's quite comfortable climbing the chair we're on, settling on the blanket while I sleep, or resting on the side of our dinner plates tasting our food with us. He's too comfortable here.

It unnerves me, and I can tell it unnerves RaeCh, too, though she brushes it off.

"Her spies are everywhere," she groans.

*They're not everywhere now,* I think. *They're just here.* "Maybe he's lonely."

"He's a thousand spiders," RaeCh replies. "He can't possibly get lonely."

"I'm not sure he works that way."

RaeCh shudders. "Whatever. It's too crowded in here now."

I remember the train station, what Clementine said. Claude hates crowds. That means he couldn't possibly be a crowd, right? Of course, what do I understand of this? Not much.

I hope he doesn't eat us in our sleep. I hope he forgets that I didn't really fight for Clementine like I was supposed to. I hope he has some amount of sympathy for RaeCh, because I think I kinda find her endearing and don't know what I'd do without her. And I worry that's the volatile relationship I wrote about as Jasper. That I just went from Ferg to Analiese to RaeCh. I tell myself this is different, but how can I know? I don't remember. But Phoebe thinks I still know, somehow. So I hope I do.

# 66

NALIESE SCOWLS AT THE SPIDERS covering the floor, the walls, the tables, bringing a darkness to the room. She frowns and daintily touches the shattered mirror, probably thinking of how much nicer the place was kept when she lived here. But she doesn't comment.

"We have to go back for Clementine," Analiese says, trying to talk sense to RaeCh. It's not working.

RaeCh rolls her eyes. "Please, let me retire in peace."

"It's not over, RaeCh."

"My plan is going swimmingly, actually. The cops have the investigative notes leading to the scene of the crime, they found a corpse there, and they have not one but two suspects that I would be more than happy to see arrested. So let them flip a coin and choose. Either way, Clementine is locked up somewhere, and I just may get a bonus of Dr. Evil being locked up, too. I'm done scheming."

"We can't leave her there. She didn't do anything."

"I'm not stopping you."

Analiese sighs. "If we go rushing in there, there's a more than likely chance that one of us isn't coming back out. And you may not care about Clementine's fate. But you care about ours. You can either rush in with us or rush in after us."

RaeChaeline sniffs. "I'll retire from caring if I have to. You make your choice. I already made mine."

"Gep wouldn't—"

"Don't! Don't you try to tell me what Gep would or wouldn't do. I know Gep better than all of you, and I'll tell you one thing. Gep won't do anything because he *can't* anymore."

Analiese huffs.

"There's no sense bringing me into the plan," RaeCh continues. "I left Clementine there. Intentionally."

She knows, somehow...what she did.

Analiese's eyes widen. She *didn't* know.

"Darn spiders told me," RaeCh adds.

"Spiders?" Analiese asks.

It sounds preposterous. Spiders don't talk. And yet, we live in a strange world I've found. Either RaeCh is losing it or Claude is...even more powerful than I realized.

RaeCh nodded. "They can't get to me, though. She deserved it."

I sit next to RaeCh. "RaeCh..." I hope I don't regret this. "You put the knife in Gep."

"For the last time, I had a plan. He was going to come back."

"Plans don't always work out," Analiese says.

"Mine do! Until her!"

Analiese looks at me, then back at RaeCh, then back at me. She clenches her fists.

"Fine. She's all yours," Analiese says—to me or Claude, I'm not sure; she's too busy glaring at RaeCh to clarify. Analiese goes to walk out, stops at the mirror again and frowns, then leaves.

"You don't have to always get it right..." I say. "...be right. You can turn off the act sometimes and just be human."

"You really think I should save...her?"

I hesitate, wondering if she'll throw me out. But in this scenario, like Phoebe had said, I know what I would do. I finally know. I nod.

She sighs and pushes to her feet. "It hurts too much." Then she hobbles to her room. Analiese was right. The mask was slipping. She's frail.

## 67

HE DARKNESS SETTLES IN. It's eerily quiet. No cops. No circus. Just me and RaeCh, with Claude watching. I wonder if it's the calm before the storm, and I wait for the storm to roll in.

Then one night, the first rumblings come.

"Max, ya there?" The radio wakes me up. It's the middle of the night, which I can only presume is Ferg trying to catch me without RaeChaeline around.

I rub the sleep out of my eyes, roll over and hope I don't squish Claude, grab the radio. "I'm here."

"...alone?"

"Relatively," I say. "Claude is here."

A pause. "Oh. Okay. Analiese has an idea. But she needs you."

Analiese? Needing me? That's new. She is staunchly a lone ranger. She does her own thing and wants others to do their own thing, just not around or with her.

"You gotta get RaeCh to the circus" he says.

"How? Why?"

I hear whispering through the radio. Then, "Tell her that Clementine escaped. Tell her the circus needs her."

I catch my breath. "Clementine escaped?"

He doesn't answer. "Tell her tomorrow morning. At dawn, wake her and tell her."

I consider that Clementine hasn't escaped. That it's a ruse to get RaeCh out. I worry what the plan for RaeCh is; I know a little about what these folks are capable of.

"At dawn, okay?" he emphasizes again.

I feel a tickle on my arm. I brush it off...a spider. I feel another tickle, and another. I realize Claude is crawling onto me, and I worry. I feel him crawl up my legs, my torso, my neck, and into my hair.

*Everyone gets out.* I feel an unnatural calm settle over me. *Everyone gets out.* "Okay," I say into the radio. "At dawn."

I set the radio down and settle back into bed. Claude doesn't leave. He covers me like a blanket, and I should be unnerved, tense; I should worry that he's out to get his companion Clementine free at any cost. Sleep should elude me, yet somehow, I drift off. Claude and I drift to sleep together.

# 68

THE HAIR DYE WAS THE EASY PART.

Raiding her wardrobe for a dress was a bit of a feat.

But it was nothing to what comes next. What was needed. What she'd been practicing her whole life for.

Patience and precision.

Each curl must be formed just so. The cheeks lifted, the eyes softened, the chin nudged just a little left of center. The form just a little more shapely, the height just a little taller. Each detail mattered.

Analiese stepped back and looked into the mirror. It wasn't her face that looked back at her.

She put her hands to her face and smiled. Oops, not quite. She squeezed the edge of her mouth just a pinch. Perfect. There was Clementine.

She twirled in her dress and stepped back further, watching Clementine reflected back at her from a dozen angles. They were ready.

# 69

 AECHAELINE WOKE TO A BANGING at the bedroom door. She pulled the covers over her face.

The banging continued, accompanied by muffled words.

Max.

She threw the covers off and climbed out of bed. Claude scrambled out of her way. He must not be ready to wake either.

She raised her arms and stretched. Can't rush the morning glow.

More banging.

She shuffled to the door and opened it. "You rang?"

"I just heard from Ferg."

She glanced out the window. Light was just barely creeping out at the horizon. "Why can't it wait 'til a normal hour of day?"

"He said Clementine's escaped."

She froze. Then turned to look at him. It had to be a trick. Claude was here. They must have gotten to Max, too.

"They need us."

But while he seemed nervous, it wasn't his lying nervous energy full of fake smiles. It was the worried nervous energy, full of shallow breathing and frantic glances, like something was out to get him. "You believe them?" she asked for good measure.

Max shrugged. "Only one way to find out."

Yes. Only one way.

Unless...there was another.

Psych Institute. Except Drs. Wise and Evil wouldn't shoot straight with her. Anything to lure them back there.

She could send Max for her, have him scope it out. Then she could tell if he was lying when he told her the answer. He was much easier to read than Wise and Evil.

"Some retirement," she said. "Can no one get by without me?"

Max shrugged again. "Who would want to?"

RaeCh laughed. Anyone. Anyone 'cept Gep. "Let's go, see what the ruckus is about. But I'm not getting anywhere close. You'll be my eyes and ears."

Max paused.

RaeCh perked up. He didn't like it. It was a trap he was setting her up for. She'd called it.

But then... "I'll do my best, but you notice more than I do. I could just get into trouble."

RaeCh sighed. False alarm. Paranoia didn't suit her retirement plans. *Can no one get by without me?*

# 70

AECHAELINE PARKS AT THE ENTRANCE to the circus. She peers out my window. "You think it's a trap?" she whispers again.

I'm glad that I technically don't know. "Your guess is better than mine."

"Always suspect a trap," she says. "Always."

"What about when you're wrong?"

"I never am," she says. "Okay, here's the plan. You go in. Scope it out and report back."

"What if I don't come back? What if I'm captured?"

"By what? Claude's miles away. Clementine is nothing without him."

I'm not convinced about that, but how can I argue. I get out of the car and approach the circus. And I don't come back.

# 71

AECH WAITED AND WATCHED FOR MAX. *He's not going to return.* But she couldn't worry about that now. She couldn't fall for whatever trap Analiese had laid to try to make her play nice.

Then, she caught a glimpse, just a brief moment, skipping down a path and behind a tent. The curls bounced just so. The dress was exactly what she'd worn a week or so ago. It couldn't be.

RaeCh blinked. It was a trick. It had to be.

But Max wasn't returning, and that had to be Clementine.

RaeCh rubbed her eyes and looked again.

Nothing.

Quiet.

She'd stood by while Clementine took Gep. She couldn't take a chance and let Clementine take Max, too. Not when he was the only one left.

It was probably a trap. But in case it wasn't...

RaeChaeline opened the car door, and jogged toward the circus. She ran behind the tent she'd seen Clementine disappear behind. It was probably a mistake, a trick. It couldn't be her.

Before her stood something new, something that hadn't been part of the circus before. Analiese was innovating. A makeshift building of some sort.

A maze.

RaeCh shivered. There was a danger to her here, somewhere. But she had to find Max before she lost him, too.

Then, a head peeked out from the maze. Clementine.

RaeCh blinked. It couldn't be her, and yet... RaeCh reached out her hand as if to touch her, to see if it was a hologram that she'd move right through, but it was much too far away still.

Clementine smiled and waved her in, then ran into the maze.

RaeChaeline's adrenaline kicked in. This was most definitely a trap, but she had to take it. She had to get to Max. And as long as she kept up the mask, as long as Clementine thought RaeCh had everything under control, she would.

RaeCh marched in after her. After Max.

It didn't take long for her to freeze. A full-length mirror faced her. She shivered and looked down.

She stumbled to the left where the path continued and walked into a wall. She saw the hands in the reflection. Strong, young, graceful, and assured hands. It was another mirror. Of course.

RaeCh took a deep breath in. Then out.

Be the perception of calm.

She glanced back at the reflection and saw the knife, dripping blood. Clasped in those assured hands. She pushed away from the wall and ran further in.

She slowed at the next turn and by habit looked up. There's her face. Young, impenetrable RaeChaeline. Confident. Smiling. No one could get past her.

RaeChaeline's lip quivered, but her reflection did not.

She made the next turn.

Old RaeChaeline. Greying, hunched, but still hard. No one would touch her. The reflection perhaps was much closer to her true form. She couldn't be sure, not after all this time.

She pressed on, realizing it wasn't a maze. It was a labyrinth. She hadn't needed to question the direction once. She just had to get through. Clementine was leading her right where she wanted her. Definitely a trap.

RaeChaeline continued, in most cases avoiding to look up, watching the ground instead. Catching glimpses of her form, new and old, glimpses of a knife and blood that she tried to forget.

And then she turned a corner and nearly stepped in a pile of dirt. She stumbled back and fell. No, not dirt. Not dirt at all. Ash puffed into a cloud in the air, and RaeChaeline coughed.

She looked at the ashes covering her hands, then looked across at the mirror. She couldn't help it, like a train wreck.

In the reflection, it wasn't campfire ash. It was RaeChaeline, young again, screaming as she holds the burnt body of Geppetto. It was his lifeless form outside the burnt clinic.

RaeChaeline let out a sob. The real one, not the reflection. She swiped her arms at her eyes, but only got ash in them. "Please, make it stop," she mumbled.

But the mirrors continued. She had to get out of here. However far it was, she had to make it through. She had to leave this place and never come back. Never feel it again.

She scrambled to her feet and stumbled forward, barely able to see through the ash and tears.

Then, she tripped on an edge in the floor that she hadn't seen. She fell forward into a wide open space, and felt the glass shatter beneath her.

Mirrors on the floor now. Mirrors surrounding her in a huge hexagon. She looked around. RaeCh young, RaeCh old, RaeCh holding a knife, holding Gep, smiling, scheming, perfect. RaeCh tried to catch her breath and couldn't. She closed her eyes and looked down, sobbing. She had to get out.

A muffled scream came out, but she realized it didn't belong to her. It didn't belong to the reflections.

"Max...? W-where are you?"

A muffled voice. He couldn't speak, but he was close by. They had him close.

She crawled forward a bit, but she had no choice. She opened her eyes. And she saw it, on the floor in front of her. The scene she'd been running from for too long.

A fire, blazing, taking over not a building, but fields. Young, assured RaeChaeline approaching Gep with a knife in her hand. "The contract calls for your death, Gep," it said.

RaeCh screamed, "No!"

But the reflection didn't hear. "I'm going to make your dreams come true."

"Not again..." RaeChaeline banged at the reflection. The reflection shattered into a dozen more. It didn't stop. "Please..."

The reflection ran the knife through Gep's body, a dozen times in a dozen different mirror fragments. Gep turned from the reflection and looked at RaeCh instead. He wasn't hurt. He was just confused why his friend would do that. Why his companion would be so sure she could bring him back.

"The burden of living..."RaeCh mumbled. "It's too much."

She heard a crash far away. Max...

She looked back at Gep again. The RaeCh reflection pushed him into the fiery fields. He burned to ash in front of her. And the reflection just smiled, confident, assured. "I'll bring you back," it said. "I can do it."

"I'm so sorry..." RaeChaeline wiped at tears on her face.

Then she felt arms, wrapping her, holding her. She looked up, relieved to see a face that wasn't her own. Max.

"What'd they do?" he said. "I'm so sorry."

"I killed him, Max."

"I know," he said. "I know."

"I thought...I-I was so sure..."

Max rested his head on her shoulder. "Wanna know a secret?" he whispered. "Gep was so sure, too. He believed in you more than you believed in yourself."

"HE BELIEVED IN YOU more than you believed in you," I say. It's a lie of course. I couldn't know what Gep thought. I know it, and RaeCh knows it.

But in this moment I don't care what Gep really thought in that moment or what he thinks now. I just think, if he's worth all that RaeCh claims (which admittedly is questionable), then he'd have to be that sort of guy. So whether he was that guy or not, I was gonna make him that guy now. Because that's the story RaeCh needed.

"But I was wrong," RaeCh said.

"Being wrong never stopped you before," Max continued. "Plan B and C, remember?" He pulled back and smiled at her. "Let's get out of here. I should have never brought you here."

RaeCh wiped her eyes and sniffled. "Darn Analiese. Knows my weakness and not afraid to use it."

He helped her up, brushed glass out of her hair and pulled a piece out of her arm. She put pressure on it, and they stumbled through, past a chair and rope on top of shattered glass where Max had broken out when he'd heard RaeCh sobbing.

And back into the circus.

Clementine stood watching, and RaeChaeline tensed. It was her.

"I'm sorry it came to this, RaeCh."

It wasn't Clementine's voice. Of course. It was... "Analiese. Quite the disguise."

"I've been practicing. We deceive too easily."

"Seems I've gotten rusty."

"You've been through a lot," the Clementine-Analiese said. "Go rest. We've got a real Clementine to rescue tomorrow."

RaeChaeline shuddered. She wanted to fight back, but the fight had been taken out of her. She wanted to yell at Clementine, at Analiese, at Max. But she was tired.

She wanted to yell at Gep for believing in her too much. She wanted to yell at herself for being so stupid, for trapping Clementine. "I can't help her escape," RaeChaeline said. "I can't be wrong again."

"What if being wrong isn't so bad sometimes?" Analiese said.

RaeChaeline squeezed Max. She hoped.

"There are some things you can't come back from." The Clementine lookalike gestured back at the hall of mirrors. "But there are some things you can. There's still time."

"...maybe," RaeChae conceded. "Take me home. Sounds like a busy day tomorrow."

Max supported RaeChaeline as they walked away. And for good measure, Max hollered back, "One day we're coming back to kick your butt, though, Clementine, Analiese, whoever you are."

# 72

RAECHAELINE PACED IN HER ROOM. Away from Max, away from the prying eyes of all except Claude.

He hovered underfoot like a puppy pouncing at the feet to play. Always almost stepped on, hopping out of the way in the nick of time as it raced back and forth with her.

She had one last plan before she'd retire. Before she could stop scheming and just live out whatever days she had left. She would come to find it a relief, she told herself. One day. It takes time.

But for now she needed the show of a lifetime. She needed Max to believe her. She needed the circus folk to buy that she was on board with their plan instead of having her own.

One last hoorah. One last caper.

*Everyone gets out.* She ran her hands through her hair and felt the spider burrowing. She breathed a deep sigh. *Everyone.*

Not this time. She flicked the spider off. Not this time.

# 73

NALIESE TOOK A DEEP BREATH. Inhale... Exhale...

She knocked on the door.

Paced.

Knocked again.

Looked back at the yard, though that's no comfort. Turned back to the door which she's suddenly thankful for.

And then, just on schedule, the door opened.

"Analiese," Mr. Trencher grumbled. "Am I dreaming?"

"If it is, it's my nightmare," she said. "I'm here for Julia."

He frowned. "Not ever, but certainly not at this ungodly hour."

Analiese gave a false smile. "Shall we ask her?"

His frown deepened even further. "Don't wake Mrs. Trencher. I'll go get her." He closed the door, and Analiese waited.

But she didn't wait long. Julia appeared at the door shortly, her hair a bit unkempt from bed, but still a pristine picture.

Analiese swallowed the bitter taste in her mouth. "I was...a bit wrong, maybe."

Julia's brows furrowed.

"Things are worse, yes, but...you belong. If you want, I mean."

"Is this an apology?"

"It's what it is," Analiese said. "Take it or leave it."

"I'll take it." Julia looked out, beyond Analiese to the statue of her likeness. "Ya know, you were right. If you hadn't pushed me out of the tent that night, Nick wouldn't be here."

"Being right isn't all it's cracked up to be."

Julia laughed.

"I could use a stagehand at the circus," Analiese said, before she could change her mind. "For the tour there will be lots to learn, lots to do. We could figure it out together. You, Nick, and I."

Julia pursed her lips. "I'm not that person anymore."

"Not an act, maybe. But you're still one of us. You'll always be one of us. It was the end of something, but it wasn't the end of that."

Julia touched her forehead, that nervous tic she had.

Analiese fiddled with her fingers, that nervous tic she had. "Forget it. We'll be fine." Analiese turned to walk away.

"You will," Julia said. "You'll be fine either way. I'll think about it, though. Thank you."

Analiese nodded, got out a dry "yeah," but didn't turn back. She kept walking.

# 74

 **BLINK AWAKE.** Claude has come to rest on my chest. I move gently so as not to disturb him too quickly. A tarantula sized spider leads the way, nudging the other spiders awake and off of me.

"Morning," I whisper.

*Today's the day.*

"Everyone gets out," I remind him.

He's in and on the car before me and RaeCh get in. She's still haggard, but she's here. That's something.

"What's the plan?" I ask.

"I was gonna ask you."

"Me?"

RaeCh shrugs. "I'm just along for the ride."

What would I do in this scenario?

Ferg is a block away and waves. I wave, and realize I won't remember it. I'll remember him, probably, but not the wave. Too close.

Too weird.

We pull into the parking lot and see the circus crew. But that's not all. They're hunkered around their car, forlorn. Things already aren't going to plan.

The cops are at the doorway, leading Clementine out in handcuffs while Dr. Evil and Dr. Wise look on.

RaeCh perks up. *Don't get too excited*, I hope.

We climb out of the car and leave the door open for Claude to spill out.

"What's the plan now?" Nick asks.

"Everyone gets out," I say. "That's as far as I got."

Analiese nods. (Who, by the way, is back to her usual non-Clementine self, though I swear something looks slightly off, and I wonder if it's my imagination or if she missed a spot.)

RaeCh jumps in. "I got this one. I can get her out."

Julia touches Analiese's hand as she fiddles with her fingers. They exchange glances.

"Trust me, for old time's sake," RaeCh says. She wearily approaches the officers, and I just hope she looks more young and spry to them than to us. I hope they perceive her differently. I hope she has her armor for whatever she has planned.

And she must. We watch as she speaks to them, as they look between Clementine and her. We watch her stretch her hands out. And they handcuff her, too. She turns and smiles assuredly at me.

Phoebe gasps. Nick puts his hand over his mouth. My mouth opens, but it's too late. They're putting them both in the vehicle. And none of us had planned for that. None of us know what to do.

# 75

HE COPS COULDN'T MAKE HEADS OR TAILS of the testimonies.

More often than not, the easy path, the path you just happened across and travel down, ends up leading to the answer. But this time the easy path kept vanishing, or in this case became two paths diverging.

Both RaeChaeline and Clementine were persons of interest. Both of them could recite the details of what happened, just with a different main character, a different murderer. Both of them knew the body was killed months prior, not in the fire, at least not this one.

"I did it," RaeChaeline said. "I drove a knife into him in the chaos of the circus fire. You can't arrest her for it."

"I did it," Clementine said. "I drove a knife into him in the chaos of the circus fire. You can't arrest her for it."

Separate rooms, but identical testimonies, word for word, no matter how many times they asked or in which way.

It was as if they'd scripted it all ahead of time, but they couldn't have. It's as if they could hear and mimic each other's words, even though they were separated. (No one noticed the spider crawling about in the corner.) And the evidence pointed as equally both ways or neither.

The case was just as confusing as before in a new way. The case was being set aside, a cold case once again. They were both being released, one of them likely a murderer. But there was nothing they could do, except wait and hope new evidence would come to light before the killer chose to strike again.

"The evidence could very easily have taken one over the other if just one of them turned," one officer said. "We just need one to break."

"They're not breaking," Jenkins responded.

"Can you imagine belonging to something like that? Creepy."

# 76

THEY RELEASE THEM BOTH. EVENTUALLY.

I don't understand what happened in there. RaeCh said she'd get Clementine out, and somehow she did. RaeCh looks confused. "What'd ya do that for?" she asks Clementine.

Clementine smirks. "Everyone gets out, remember. Besides, jail isn't your toybox."

I don't understand what's happening, but I'm relieved to have RaeCh back. I run up and hug her, and she laughs.

"Just to be clear," RaeCh says to Clementine. "We're not even."

"No one gets off that easy," Clementine says and laughs.

I'm not sure if they're talking about Clementine "killing" Gep or RaeCh locking up Clementine or some new third situation with the cops. I'm not sure it matters to them either way. One or both owe the other, when the time comes.

# Epilogue

E WOULDN'T WANT A CHURCH, RaeCh had said. The circus was his sacred space in the end.

So they stood in the big top, facing each other in a circle. Except Ferg, who stood back, peering through the entry with his radio.

"Thank you all for coming." RaeChaeline cleared her throat. "You may not all have liked Gep, but I'm not sure that matters at funerals."

A couple folks let out a nervous laugh.

RaeChaeline continued. "Gep was...a dreamer. He never settled with the world as it was; he only saw what it could be. The future is a bit dimmer without him in it."

"Gep made a place for us," Analiese added in. "He made us home."

RaeChaeline looked up and nodded, her eyes glistening.

"He gave me a chance to matter," Sullivan murmured.

"The system was flawed," Nick said. "But he helped me face my fear when no one else could."

Julia tensed and folded her arms against her chest.

Phoebe gave a light smile. "I don't remember much, but from what I do remember he was a patient optimist. No matter the circumstances, they could always get better, and he wasn't in a hurry about it."

A silence stretched out as each individual considered Gep's mark on them, some memories pleasant and many otherwise.

"He was running," Ferguson's voice crackled in through the radio. "He was running from what he couldn't face, and he never got a chance to change."

Max clasped RaeCh's hand as her breathing quickened. RaeCh pursed her lips.

"It's not fair," Ferg continued. "And it's not fair that I see the same man when I look in the mirror instead of someone different, and I gotta live with that now."

"Well, we all have our own perspective," RaeChaeline said. "He was a friend. A poor one, but a true one. He had his ways."

Max jumped in. "I never met Gep. I mean, that I remember. And yet he left his mark on each of us. He intertwined the world he dreamed of with our world, and each of us bear that now. His life is proof that each of us leaves something behind within one another."

Clementine smiled at Max. "See, a poet," she whispered.

Max scrunched his nose.

Clementine spoke aloud then. "I, too, never met Gep. Claude had plenty to say about him. As RaeChaeline said, a dreamer. As Ferg said, a runner. He hadn't found what he was looking for yet, but he wasn't giving up."

Analiese wasn't watching Clementine, or any of the folks waxing not-so-eloquent. She was studying Julia, whose face grew harder with each word.

"And if that's all people have to say about us when our time comes," Analiese interjected. "That we chased after dreams and bulldozed their lives in the process, that's not a world to dream for." Julia looked up at Analiese, who continued. "Gep had his admirable qualities, as do we all. And he's a cautionary tale that the most important part can fall through the cracks. I've not been much better, and I'm not yet. But maybe because of him, I will be."

Analiese nodded at Julia, sending a message that didn't bear words. An understanding of what had passed and what the future might hold instead. Not quite a promise, but a hope.

RaeChaeline cleared her throat. "May we all have better funerals than this one." She lifted a piece of paper. "This is the first contract, and the last."

Nick picked up the lantern, and held it out to RaeChaeline. She placed the contract into the flame. As it lit, she drew it back and held it up. The flames reflected the tears dripping down her face as each person remembered one or more fires that changed their life.

In mere seconds, the flames approached RaeChaeline's hand, and she dropped the remains and stepped back. She swiped the tears from her cheeks and chin. The flames fizzled out.

RaeChaeline stooped to the ground, touched the hot ash, and whispered, "You'll always have my heart."

They all stood in silence as they each said goodbye to Gep in their own way.

Finally, RaeChaeline stood and spoke again. "What now?"

"Indeed," Clementine said. "What now?"

THAT'S WHAT WE ALL WONDER. What now?

We don't all figure it out at once.

Analiese already had it figured out. She starts her circus tour with Nick by her side and Julia promising to visit. Even the Sullivan guy is excited to be part of something big. The cops continue to watch the circus closely, but Analiese doesn't mind being the distraction. Nothing to hide, she says.

Clementine and Claude catch a ride and travel in the circus wagons to the circus's first stop. Then they venture off to explore the world on their own. They haven't figured out how to get around, but they will.

Phoebe and Julia decide to move into an apartment together, to figure out what life might look like for them without relying on other people. They don't have it all figured out yet, but who does?

Sylas meanders wherever he so pleases, like he tends to do. I guess picking up and putting down Clementine's "toyboxes" each moment, like they're all on loan.

Ferg keeps his apartment and his life, absent one Jasper. (I once asked him how in the world he comes by money to pay for an apartment or anything. He said being so forgettable pays. I don't think I want to know what that means.) We stay in touch by radio. We're kinda, maybe, sorta friends. We're not sure.

RaeChaeline settles in at the mansion, "looking after it for the Trenchers," she claims. She's gonna try this whole retirement thing, and I don't think she'll last long.

"And what about you?" RaeCh asks.

Good question. What about me? What would I do in this scenario? My whole life ahead of me for the taking. "I don't know," I say. I told you we don't have it all figured out.

"You know, I have a thought," RaeCh says.

"What? You do?"

RaeCh nods. "You'd make an impeccable private investigator."

I laugh.

"Really," she says.

"Ya think?"

"Absolutely."

I think about it, then decide what I'd do in this situation. "Only if you help."

RaeCh looked up just in time to catch the sparkle in his eye. She sniffed, tapped her fingers on the table in front of her. "I may consider some amount of consulting. But I charge a hefty fee."

THE END

## ~Acknowledgments~

To Batman, who showed we can conquer our fear of terrifying creatures by embracing them as part of our identity.

(...it didn't work.)

## ~Liked it? Or didn't?~

The book world needs you!

...

Lend the superpowers of an honest review on Goodreads, Amazon, your social media, wherever. Your reviews help readers choose a book they'll enjoy, and help authors find their readers. It's a win-win-win-win-win-win... You get the picture.

...

*~Be the reviewer~*
*~the world needs today~*

## ~The party ain't over!~

Tag your fanfiction, fanart, & headcanon:
**#UnfixedWorld**

...

Send it my way:
*Website:* AmyLSauder.com
*Facebook:* /AmyLSauder
*Twitter:* @AmyLSauder
*Instagram:* @AmyLSauderCreations

# About the Author

Amy L. Sauder is a creative and a writer of introspective psychological stories, including the Unfixed series and the quirky mystery "I Know You Like a Murder." She lives on the edge of an enchanted wood with her husband Josh and her mannequin Delilah.

www.ingramcontent.com/pod-product-compliance
Ingram Content Group UK Ltd.
Pitfield, Milton Keynes, MK11 3LW, UK
UKHW040255200225
455254UK00004B/188

9 781732 353046